Swimming to the Moon

JANE ELSON

HODDER CHILDREN'S BOOKS

First published in Great Britain in 2016 by Hodder and Stoughton

3 5 7 9 10 8 6 4 2

A CIP catalogue record for this book is available from the British Library

ISBN 978 1 444 92775 7

Typeset in Egyptian 505 by Avon DataSet Ltd,
Bidford-on-Avon, Warwickshire

Printed and bound in Great Britain by Clays Ltd, St Ives plc

The paper and board used in this book are from well-managed forests
and other responsible sources.

Hodder Children's Books
An imprint of
Hachette Children's Group
Part of Hodder & Stoughton
Carmelite House
50 Victoria Embankment
London EC4Y 0DZ

An Hachette UK Company
www.hachette.co.uk

For anyone who's ever been told
they can't

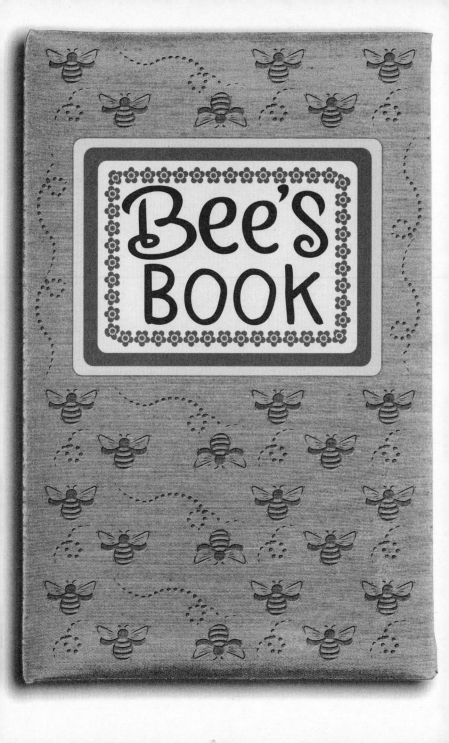

My dearest darling Bee,

When you read this I will have gone from this earth, but if you look up at the night's sky, the brightest, twinkliest star is me, shining my love down to you.

This book is my final gift to you, my own unique girl. I have filled its pages with the wisdom of the honeybee.

Knowing you and watching you grow has brought me pleasure as sweet as any honey. My deepest sorrow is that I shall not see you grow into the wise woman with dazzling style that I know you will become, the seeds of which are sown deep, deep inside you, already starting to bloom.

As the poet William Blake said: 'The busy bee has no time for sorrow.' So don't cry tears for me. Get on and live your life.

But, should you have moments of sadness, write them in this book and imagine you are sending them to me.

Remember — every bee in the hive has a purpose and a reason for living:

The queen to lay eggs.

The drone to serve the queen.

The worker to pollinate flowers and make honey.

Find your purpose in life, Bee.

I have so loved the time we spent together, watching old Judy Garland and Marilyn Monroe films — especially **The Wizard of Oz** and **Some Like It Hot**. Your face would light the room as the stories unfolded. Just as Dorothy did in **The Wizard of Oz**, you must follow your yellow brick road to your destiny.

My love for you is bigger than the sky and all the stars put together.

Your Great-Gran Beatrix xxxxx

Dear Great-Gran Beatrix,

I am feeling sad, so I thought I should write you a letter in my bee book.

Mum and Dad are arguing, so I am hiding in my bedroom to get away from all the shouting.

I miss you a million more times than the number of all the bees in all the hives in the whole wide world.

It makes me happy again when I look at all the wondrous things we made for my bedroom — the film-star wall with the clapperboard in the middle that says 'The Life of Bee: Take 1'. And the pictures of Marilyn Monroe and Judy Garland, who you know are my all-time best-ever actresses. When Marilyn Monroe acted, it was like a light shone from inside her and reached out to the whole wide world — wasn't it, Great-Gran Beatrix? I loved it when you used to tell me that the day I was born, I lit up your world with my sunshine eyes.

Marilyn had grace and poise and a wiggly-waggly walk, but, Great-Gran Beatrix, I have something to tell you ... Madame Bertha of Madame Bertha's

Ballet and Tap Academy says *I do not* have grace and poise. She says I have the elegance of a rugby player and that I am not the type of child she encourages to enrol at Madame Bertha's Ballet and Tap Academy. You remember how she used to make us curtsey at the end of every class but I always wobbled and my bottom would stick out? Well, last Thursday I wobbled so much I fell over, and the whole class laughed. Madame Bertha turned purple and shouted at me.

'It's not my fault that I don't have a curtseying type of bottom!' I shouted back.

She asked me to leave.

Which you know, Great-Gran Beatrix, is absolutely fine by me because I hate dancing, and acting is my thing. I'm a brilliant actress. I'm very proud of my virtual scrapbook of expressions for any occasion, which I keep in my imagination and can show on my face. Just like Marilyn Monroe.

I don't know if it's true, but I saw on *Film Stars - Fact or Fiction* that Marilyn's walk came from the day she broke a bit of the heel of one of her shoes. She liked the way it made her walk wiggly-waggly and from then on she always had one heel shorter than the other. I am always breaking my shoes or losing them but this does not give me grace and a film-star walk. It just gets me into Big Trouble. I have:

A single fluffy slipper (I have looked under my bed a million times for the other one).

One pair of trainers (with no laces).

One pair of leather boots – the ones I got for Christmas (the zips broke, so now they flap when I walk).

One broken summer sandal – I fell down the stairs in them and the straps snapped. (PS: Why do people always say 'be careful' after you have fallen down? What's the good in that?)

So, now I stick to wearing my black DM boots and my favourite stripy socks, which you said, Great-Gran Beatrix, give me dazzling style.

I miss you.

Bee xxxx

Dear Great-Gran Beatrix,

I can see all the pictures we stuck on the wall of Marilyn Monroe and Judy Garland reflected in my dressing-table mirror. It's Christmas Day, and *The Wizard of Oz* is on TV again. Mum made a special tea and wanted to watch the film with me. But I can't watch it without you, Great-Gran Beatrix, I just can't – so I ran upstairs.

It's nearly finished now, but I can hear Judy Garland acting as Dorothy from my room. Oh, Great-Gran Beatrix, wasn't she just brilliant?

When she started singing 'Somewhere Over the Rainbow', my heart stopped and I was inside every note. I found myself creeping out of my bedroom to sit on the stairs to listen. And when Dorothy said to the Scarecrow, 'I'll miss you most of all,' I found myself whispering it with her, except I said, 'I'll miss you most of all, Great-Gran Beatrix,' because I do. My life's just not the same without you.

Anyway, Mum's calling me downstairs – I'd better go.

Bee xxxxx

PS: Me again! I wish you were here so I could show you the picture Mum has just drawn me of the famous white dress Marilyn wore in the film

The Seven Year Itch. She said she thought it would cheer me up.

You know how much I love, love, LOVE this dress, with its teeny, tiny pleats and swirly, swirly skirts. It's just so beautiful. I would not let the wind blow up my skirt to show my knickers though. I do not even like showing my knickers when I change for PE. Bee xxx

PPS: By the way, just in case you're wondering, Dad didn't get me a phone for Christmas. Even though I begged and pleaded.

Dear Great-Gran Beatrix,

My hatstand, with all the hats you bought me on every birthday since I was a little girl, is my very favourite thing in the world. You know how I treasure each and every hat — my trilby, my top hat, my bowler, my beret, my deerstalker. But today, I am sad because I have been looking at the empty peg where one special hat should be. And it's empty because of a promise I broke; a lie that I told.

I'm sorry, Great-Gran Beatrix, I can't write about this any more — it hurts too much.

Sending an extra big kiss up to the stars.

Love you,

Bee xxxxx

1

Just call me Bee. Please, please call me that. If you call me Beatrix Daffodil Tulip Chrysanthemum Rose Edwards I won't answer you. I am not being rude or unfriendly, or insolent, as Mrs Partridge, my teacher, calls me. I just don't like my name. Well – would you?

Beatrix was the name of my great-grandmother. I like that name because it can be shortened to Bee, and it's the name of the person who I happened to love most in the whole world when she lived on planet earth.

It's the other names I don't like. Neither does my mum.

'HOW CAN YOU CALL YOUR DAUGHTER AFTER A BUNCH OF HALF-DEAD FLOWERS

THAT YOU GOT CHEAP FROM A PETROL STATION?' she always screams at Dad when they have a row. Which happens a lot.

Daffodil, tulip, chrysanthemum and rose were the names of the flowers in the bouquet that Dad brought to the hospital to say sorry to Mum when he missed me being born. So you can understand why she gets angry with him. She probably doesn't want to be reminded about this every time she hears my whole name.

The story goes that Dad stopped off at the Dog and Duck pub on the way to the hospital and lost track of time. Mum wanted to call me Sarah, but Dad registered my birth down at the town hall without her knowing. She didn't talk to him for four weeks and four days when he told her what he'd done.

At least the house would have been quiet when they weren't talking to each other – apart from me screaming of course. I bet I was loud. Everyone's loud in this house.

This morning is no exception. I'm on the search for marmalade, and as I pull open the fridge door and stare at the empty shelf where the jar should be, one of the fridge magnets slides off with a clang, sending the map of our village I drew at junior school fluttering to the floor.

Footsteps clatter down the rickety stairs. I go to take a bite of toast but Mum runs into the kitchen, still in her PJs, her red tousled hair standing on end, and swipes the plate from under my nose.

'Bee, look at the time – it's eight forty-five! Go on, get to school now, before your father sees you and starts shouting.'

I duck around Mum, snatch the toast off the plate, take a bite and grab my blue school bag from the hall – all within the space of about five seconds. I think that's pretty spectacular of me, considering I am the worst person at sports in the history of planet earth. Can't catch. Can't throw. Even if my hands were as big as an oak tree, if you threw a ball straight at me it would still go sailing over the tops of my finger-branches, into the sky.

I yank my long yellow and black stripy socks up over my knees, squeeze my feet into my black DMs and tie the laces into a scrambled knot, then I give myself a quick glance in the mirror on the way out of the front door. My reflection gapes back at me – long red hair, freckles and a face COVERED IN TOAST CRUMBS! Oops. I wipe my mouth on the back of my hand and then I remember – hat! I need one of my special hats to add some style to my boring grey school uniform. But I hear Dad stomping around upstairs, muttering to himself. There is no way I am going up there, not even if I double-dare myself.

Then I spy something black wedged behind the umbrella stand. Hurrah! It's one of my all-time favourites – the black beret, made of the softest lambswool, which Great-Gran Beatrix gave me for my seventh birthday. I scoop it up and put it on, adjusting it in the mirror so it sits at a slight angle. I'm wearing it 'with jaunty style', as Great-Gran Beatrix used to say.

'BEE, GET TO SCHOOL!' yells Mum.

As the door of our little house in Duck Street bangs behind me, I shut my eyes, as I do every morning when I step out of my front door. The warmth of the sun and a gentle breeze kiss my eyelids and cheeks at the same time. A very good day for the bees to collect their nectar. I hear a door slamming inside the house. On your marks, get set, go, and Mum and Dad are off again . . .

'WHY IS THAT GIRL ALWAYS LATE FOR SCHOOL?' shouts Dad so loudly, it echoes into the street.

'HAS IT OCCURRED TO YOU THAT IF WE WEREN'T BUSY YELLING AT EACH OTHER ONE OF US COULD HAVE GOT BEE OFF TO SCHOOL ON TIME! YOU ALWAYS HAVE TO HAVE THINGS YOUR OWN WAY!' screams Mum.

'I DON'T!' bellows Dad.

'YOU DO – LOOK AT THE RIDICULOUS NAME YOU GAVE YOUR OWN DAUGHTER.'

'WHY DO YOU HAVE TO BRING BEE'S NAME INTO EVERY ARGUMENT? YOU'RE LIKE A BROKEN RECORD,' Dad yells.

And it's at that moment I realise I don't have my key. I'm always dropping it. I turn round with my eyes still shut, not opening them till I am peeping through the letter box. I can see my front door key lying on the carpet.

'Mum, Dad, please open the door,' I call, but they are too busy shouting to hear me.

They never hear me. I wish Great-Gran Beatrix were here. Sometimes my bones ache, I miss her so much.

I give up, take a deep breath, clutching at the tiny bit of bravery that's hiding inside me, and force my eyes to stay open as I slowly turn around.

There it is, right in front of me, the Rise and Shine Happy Care Home for Older People, where Great-Gran Beatrix lived. My breath catches on my tonsils, like it does every single time I think about her sitting in her armchair. This is why I keep my eyes closed, so I'm not reminded—

'BEE, BEE!'

Linford and Millie, two of the old people who live in the Rise and Shine Happy Care Home for Older People, and my great-gran's dearest friends, call to me as they jog out of the front door in matching tracksuits. They are mad old people who go bungee jumping and climb mountains and do other daring activities to raise money for the Rise and Shine Happy Care Home.

I spy Matilda, another of Great-Gran Beatrix's special friends, through the window. She's playing the piano and singing 'Tea for Two'. According to Mum, she once played the piano for the Queen.

Sid, a tiny bald old man in spectacles, who used to be a window cleaner, is squeezing out a big sponge over a bucket of soapy water. 'Come for tea soon, Bee,' he calls.

'Tomorrow,' I lie. 'I'm late for school,' I truth.

The old people ask me to come to tea every time they see me, but I can't. I just can't.

I wave at Mabel, who used to be a bingo caller, but she doesn't see me. She is too busy weeding the garden and muttering bingo numbers to herself.

'We'll see you sooner than you think . . .' Linford and Millie call from across the road.

I want to ask them what they mean, but they've already gone, jogging up the road.

So I turn and run away from my memories, all elbows and knees everywhere. As I run along Duck Street I can see the gardens and allotments belonging to the Rise and Shine Happy Care Home, full of vegetables and beautiful flowers for the bees to pollinate.

Our village is shaped like a number eight, only the circle at the bottom, which is where I live, is called *Little* Ash because it's smaller than the circle at the top, Ashton. There is only one single road leading out of Ashton to the rest of the world. The big problem is, the only way I can get to my school, which is beyond the woods in the big circle, is by crossing a crooked bridge over a deep, swirling, hateful, terrifying river. There is no other way. That's the only bad thing though. Apart from that, the whole village is surrounded by forest, and fields and grassy paths. It's like we're being hugged by nature.

I've always thought the houses in Duck Street are like those painted wooden Russian dolls – the ones that open, and inside there's a smaller doll, and inside that one is an even smaller doll, and so on. You line them up next to each other with the mama doll at one end, going down till you reach the tiny baby. As I run up my street from my house – the tiny little baby doll – I watch the houses grow, each one bigger than the last, until I reach the big mama house that belongs to—

I trip and hear a snigger.

'If it isn't Usain Bolt!' screeches a voice that rips into my daydreams.

I look up to see my arch-enemy and bendy tap-dancing freak, Chrystal Kelly, sitting as smugly as can be in the tree outside her house, smirking at me. It used to be *our* tree, where we would sit, swinging our legs, whispering secrets. Now, Chrystal just plagues me in the playground, challenging me to dance-offs and laughing at my moves.

'You run like a stick insect that's had an electric shock,' she calls.

As I pick myself up from the ground, Chrystal's front door opens and out steps her dad, Mayor Kelly, with his close-cropped black hair, dark overcoat and mayor's golden livery glinting round his neck. His two stooges – as Great-Gran Beatrix used to call them – short, fat Burt and tall, lanky Alfie, trot out after him. Wherever Mayor Kelly goes, those two are always close by.

I don't know why but I shiver as I watch them stand in the corner of the front garden in a huddle, looking like school bullies chatting dark secrets. I feel Chrystal's eyes boring into me. I glance up at the tree, and our eyes meet for a glimmer of a second before she tosses her golden curls and looks away.

'Chrystal darling, get down from that tree. You must save your energy for swimming training this evening,' calls Mrs Kelly, as she totters through the doorway dressed in a white trouser suit and very high heels. She is carrying Mitzi, her chihuahua, who is dressed in a matching white trouser suit. Mrs Kelly and Mitzi like to coordinate at all times. Mitzi yaps as Mrs Kelly *tip-taps* towards her black Porsche.

Chrystal does a spectacular leap out of

the tree and lands in the splits with her arms in the air.

'Nice one, Chrystal!' Lorna, the nanny, steps out of the house behind Mrs Kelly, with baby Daniel in her arms.

Chrystal jumps up and runs to give her baby brother a kiss, shakes out her hair, pirouettes to the Porsche then scrambles into the back seat, ignoring me.

Daniel's the cutest little baby boy in the world, with his mop of black curly hair and big blue eyes. I miss playing with him now that Chrystal and I are enemies.

Because Chrystal's dad is the mayor, they live in the biggest house in the whole village and can afford nannies and millions of dance lessons at Madame Bertha's Ballet and Tap Academy and other activities. I used to do one ballet class a week at Madame Bertha's till I was asked to leave.

Now, it's not that long a walk from here to school, but I'm still going to be late and in trouble and I'll have to go over the CROOKED

BRIDGE AND THAT RIVER, and walk through hundreds of trees and things to get there.

A lift would be nice, even in my enemy's car.

I dig deep into my virtual scrapbook of expressions that I keep in my brain, to find the perfect one for this occasion. I decide to go for *the clever, worried schoolgirl who does not like to miss lessons* face. I wonder how often Marilyn Monroe and Judy Garland had to dig into their scrapbooks of expressions when they were acting their parts.

I bite my bottom lip to create a good *desperate to get to school* look then, as Mrs Kelly starts up the car, I think *desperate to get to school* thoughts. The car backs out of the drive, turns, and as it gets closer, I smile and hold out my hand to open the door . . . But instead of stopping to allow me in, Mrs Kelly manages to find the only muddy puddle and drives straight through it.

DIDN'T SHE EVEN SEE ME STANDING THERE? Of course, there is Chrystal laughing at me from the back seat, holding Mitzi up and making her wave her little paw at me.

I give her my *I don't care, I am a film star* look, as I whisk out my bumblebee mirror to check the damage. I don't look like a film star at all. I look like a wet, muddy schoolgirl with soggy toast crumbs stuck to her cardigan.

And then I feel it. The elephant sits down on my chest and I begin to wheeze. Oh no! This always happens when I've been running and I'm late and Chrystal . . . and, well, everything. I dig in my bag for my Easy Breathe asthma inhaler. Where is it? Where is it? Where is it? I feel the inhaler, hiding underneath my pencil case.

I take off the cap and shake it. Then I breathe out and push the inhaler into my mouth, one sharp breath in, and as the powder hits the back of my throat, I keep on breathing in, just like Nurse Jessica told me to. I hold my breath for one, two, three, four, five, six, seven, eight, nine, ten and then breathe out again.

'Counting makes things better, my little chick,' Nurse Jessica used to say. 'It always makes things better.'

The wheeze and the rattle stops as the elephant climbs off my chest. I have lots of good days where I don't need my inhaler at all. Then I have my bad days, such as today, usually when Mum and Dad shout at each other.

I turn into the road that cuts through the woods and walk slowly towards the bridge. Even though I am late, I can't make my legs go any faster, I just can't, because the swirling waters are getting closer and closer. I hear them calling me.

I reach the bridge and suddenly I am three years old and I'm having a picnic in the woods by the lake with Great-Gran Beatrix. I call, 'Look at me, I'm dancing!' and I'm twirling round and round and round, faster and faster. 'Look at me, look at me, I'm da—' And as the icy water hits me and sucks me under, Great-Gran Beatrix's scream reaches the sky. Down, down, down I go, the waters pulling me, sucking me down to their depths to keep me there for ever. Then strong arms encircle me and start pulling me up, up, up to the surface and as the air brushes my cheeks I realise it's Linford, Great-Gran Beatrix's dear friend.

The memory mist disappears. I hear Nurse Jessica's voice say, '*Counting makes things better, my little chick, it always makes things better,*' so I play the game I play every day. I step off the road and hide behind a tree while I make sure that no cars are coming over the crooked bridge that crosses the river. Then I have to hop over the bridge in twenty-five hops exactly. If I do this then the water won't get me. I know it sounds silly, but it's my thing and I just have to do it.

There are no cars. I close my eyes. I stand on one leg. 1, 2, 3 – the waters are gurgling – 4, 5, 6, 7 – they are getting louder – 8, 9 – and louder – 10, 11 – and louder – 12, 13. I'm halfway – 14, 15. I shudder at the feel of my damp shirt and mud-splattered cardigan against my arms. 16, 17, 18, 19 – nearly there – 20, 21 – nearly in Ashton – BEEEEEEP! My eyes snap open; a red car is coming straight at me. The driver slams on his brakes. I wobble and grab the wooden railing; the spray from the gurgling river splashes my face. The car driver winds down the window, shouts rude words and drives off.

I didn't make it. I close my eyes and hop – 22, 23, 24, 25 – but my legs are wobbling. It doesn't count cos I didn't do it in one go. I'll have to do it again and panic starts to fill me inside, rising and rising, cos it means the waters will get me and—

Something soft brushes against my leg. It's a tiny grey kitten. I bend down and hold my finger out. The kitten sniffs it with his little pink nose. I scoop him up and he snuggles into my cheek and the panic vanishes.

It's then that I realise I am standing right opposite the witch's wagon.

2

On the other side of the bridge, in the clearing in front of me, is Old Alice's painted wagon.

There are cats everywhere – ginger, black, white, tabby, scampering, snoozing, rolling in the dust, draped on branches of trees, drinking from puddles, mewing, mauling, spitting, hissing, playing. Marmaduke, the school caretaker's ginger tom, is having a stand-off staring match with a huge hissing tabby. This is not Marmaduke's territory.

I put the kitten down and he scampers away, not getting far before a large black and grey cat catches him, bites the scruff of his neck and carries him off. I straighten up and study Old Alice's wagon for signs of life.

They say she's a witch. I *know* she's a witch. She shouts curses at people who cross her, and she feeds the feral cats that hide behind the wheels of her red wagon. She's not often seen. I haven't seen her for months.

Before we were enemies, Chrystal and I used to dare each other to touch the wheels of the wagon. It was our most scariest thing to do ever.

Then came the day of the double-dare and the double-double-dare.

'Go on,' Chrystal said. 'Double-dare you to run all the way round the wagon.'

You can say no to a dare, but a double-dare HAS to be done. It's the rules.

'Over the rainbow and back,' I said. Which was our special, most secret thing we used to say to each other, ever since the first time Great-Gran Beatrix tucked us up on the sofa together in her rainbow blanket when we had chicken pox. We ate toasted teacakes dripping with butter and watched *The Wizard of Oz*.

And I did it. I actually did. I ran all the way round, and I kept on running down a little path in front of me and all the way to the Promise Tree, the ginormous oak tree with the ancient myth written on it that declares that there must always be a traveller living in the clearing in the woods or the bees will swarm. And that's when I saw them for the first time – the beehives. I forgot my double-dare and just stopped and stared.

Old Alice was in the middle of a cloud of honeybees, muttering away to them. I couldn't believe my eyes. Then she looked up and saw me standing there watching her.

'Come closer, child. Help me charm the bees?' she said, beckoning me with her long bony finger. 'Gently does it so you don't make 'em cross.' The bees were dancing in the air around her.

And I wanted to with all my heart, I really did. I wanted to charm the bees with Old Alice, but instead I just ran, ran, ran, back round the wagon, to where Chrystal, my old friend/new enemy, was standing.

'There're hives at the end of the path,' I puffed. 'I saw them.'

Chrystal went white – she is scared as scared can be of getting stung.

And I said in my best dramatic voice ever, 'OLD ALICE IS DOWN THERE WITH THE BEES. I SAW HER WITH MY OWN EYES AND SHE LOOKED RIGHT AT ME!'

We both screamed and hid behind a tree and watched, trembling, as Old Alice walked up the steps of her wagon and disappeared inside.

But I didn't breathe a word to Chrystal that I had actually seen Old Alice charming the bees. It felt like it was Old Alice's secret that I had stumbled upon and not mine to tell.

It was my turn. 'Double-double-dare,' I said and giggled my double-double-dare, WHICH CAN NEVER EVER BE TURNED BACK ON, AS IT IS THE HIGHEST LEVEL OF ALL DARES, into Chrystal's ear.

'Go on,' I added.

'No,' she said, 'you go first. I usually always go first.'

'That's cos you're bossy,' I said.

'I am quicker and faster than you, Bee,' she said.

'We'll go together,' I said.

We had to run round Old Alice's wagon and down the path towards the Promise Tree and touch a beehive, ACTUALLY TOUCH IT. With blindfolds on our eyes.

'Carefully, though,' I said. 'We mustn't hurt the bees.'

'Over the rainbow and back,' we shouted together and blindfolded ourselves with our school ties.

And we were stumbling and giggling and bumping into each other, only then I went the wrong way. I was sure I was going past Old Alice's wagon but instead I was heading deep into the wood. Then I heard the scream. I ripped off my tie and ran towards it.

I ran towards the Promise Tree and there was Chrystal screaming and flapping. 'YOU RAN AWAY AND LEFT ME,' she cried. 'YOU CHEATED.'

Old Alice suddenly appeared from behind the Promise Tree, her fingers entwined with the twigs of the oak. My heart stopped beating.

'Stay still,' she whispered. 'Don't scare the bees.'

But Chrystal DID NOT LISTEN – she never listens. She ran away screaming and a beautiful bee got caught in her hand and stung her thumb. And then it died.

We were meant to be gentle and not scare the bees. Chrystal was my bestest friend on the whole of planet earth, until that day.

Ever since the double-double-dare, there's another thing I have to do. Like I have to do my twenty-five hops over the bridge, whenever I pass Old Alice's wagon I must stand still, close my eyes, count to three and listen to the song of the bees as they hum. It's because I feel heartbroken about the one that died just cos of our stupid double-double-dare.

You see, I am not scared of bees like Chrystal is; I love them. In the spring and the summer I can hear their song vibrating through the air. In the winter, I just pretend I can hear it – which is nearly as good.

I stand there to respect the bees.

Even though I am already late for school, I still have to do my thing. I walk slowly, slowly towards Old Alice's wagon. I stand in front. I close my eyes. I feel a breeze against my cheek. I start to count,

'One.'

I hear a robin sing.

'Two.'

A hand grabs my arm.

My eyes snap open – Old Alice is standing in front of me, her face up close to mine.

'Please,' she starts. 'Please . . .'

'Threeeee.' I have to finish my thing.

'Please—'

'THREE!' I scream. 'THREEEEEEEEEE.'

She is still holding on to my arm, so I struggle out of my cardigan and jackknife away from her, leaving her clutching my cardie. I run through the woods and up, up, up the road, through Ashton Square, past the town clock tower showing TEN PAST NINE – I am in such trouble – past the statue of Mayor Kelly, and turn right into school.

3

My old friend the elephant plonks himself back on to my chest. Wheezing and rattling, I scrabble for my inhaler and breathe in, hold for ten, and out, until the elephant vanishes.

I slip through the door and sneak past nosy Miss Willow, the school secretary, in her office. I think I've almost done it, when I hear tutting. I turn. Miss Willow is standing in the middle of the corridor.

'Take that ridiculous hat off, Bee. Where's your cardigan? And look at those boots and socks – you look a mess! Assembly has already started.'

I give her my best *a witch stole my cardigan* look.

'Bee, don't just stand there pulling funny faces. Sneak in the back, and quietly please.'

I pull my beret off my head and stuff it in my bag. Miss Willow just doesn't get style.

I open the door a crack. I see the younger kids sitting cross-legged on the floor. Year Six sit on chairs at the back of the hall. Spying an empty chair in the back row behind Chrystal Kelly, I slither through the door. I would definitely make a good top-secret spy. But as I lower myself on to the chair, it rocks and scrapes and the whole school turns around. Chrystal smirks at me and Mr Gregory, the head teacher, stops droning on and stares right at me, his three chins wobbling.

'BEATRIXDAFFODILTULIPCHRYSANTHEMUM ROSE EDWARDS, YOU ARE LATE, AND YOU HAVE INTERRUPTED MR GREGORY'S MOST INTERESTING ASSEMBLY!' screeches Mrs Partridge, my class teacher.

The whole of Ashton Junior School laughs. Why did she have to shout out my rubbish name like that? Whenever she is angry or particularly pleased with any kid in her class, Mrs Partridge uses their whole name, even if they don't like it.

I sit up straight, try to ignore them all and look right in front of me to the stage.

I dig deep for my *I am very intelligent and am waiting for the assembly to start again* look. After a forever silence, Mr Gregory coughs and continues to drone on.

'Running in corridors – drone drone drone.

'Football match – drone drone drone.

'No mobiles – drone drone drone.

'House Cup – drone drone drone drone.'

I try to concentrate, but I can see a beautiful honeybee outside, flying from rose to rose in the garden next to the school. It's Mr Gregory's garden.

That's when three things happen all at once. The honeybee flies through the window, the door opens and a new boy enters. New Boy looks like he is most probably in Year Six, but he doesn't know we are allowed to sit on chairs and plonks himself on the floor with Year Five.

The song of the bee's buzzing sounds

beautiful over the top of Mr Gregory's droning.

Then the bee lands on Chrystal Kelly's hair. She leaps up and flaps and screams. Just like she did on the day of the double-double-dare.

'Stand still!' I shout. I simply can't bear another bee dying because it's stung Chrystal Kelly.

'Ahhh! Get it off me! Ahhhhh!' Flap flap flap flap flap.

'Yes, do stand still, Chrystal,' calls Mrs Partridge.

Lily and Alba, who surround Chrystal at all times now, like the bread of a sandwich, start screaming too.

'You're going to be stung,' screeches Lily unhelpfully, hopping on one foot and waving her hands in circles, like propellers.

'HELP, HELP, HEEEELLLLLLP,' cries Alba, pulling on her plaits.

The beautiful bee lands on the floor for a moment and Chrystal brings up her big ugly foot to stamp on it.

'DON'T HURT THE BEE!' I scream, and

I leap up and throw myself at Chrystal.

She lands on the floor with a thump.

'OH MY LEG! MISS, BEE ATTACKED ME! MRS PARTRIDGE! HELP ME!'

The hall falls silent. I scrunch up my face, hold my breath and say a thousand prayers that Chrystal Kelly did not squash the beautiful honeybee with her bum when she landed on the floor – because that would be a horrible way for the poor bee to die.

I hear a buzzing high up in the rafters of the hall. I let out my breath.

The honeybee has escaped.

'BEATRIXDAFFODILTULIPCHRYSANTHEMUM ROSE EDWARDS,' screeches Mrs Partridge, her long nose quivering. 'GO AND STAND IN THE CORNER AT THE BACK. NOW! HOW DARE YOU ATTACK CHRYSTAL AND INTERRUPT MR GREGORY'S ASSEMBLY AGAIN!' She gives the head teacher a most sickening smile.

'BEATRIX, YOU WILL COME TO MY OFFICE AFTER ASSEMBLY,' Mr Gregory bellows, his chins wobbling.

As I stomp off to the corner, by the window, I feel a pair of eyes follow me. It's the new boy, who has found a seat in the back row. I lean against the wall and stare back at him just for a second. His jet black hair is sticking up as if it has been electrocuted by a million volts and his school uniform looks like it's been trampled on by a thousand rhinoceroses. His deep blue eyes hitchhike into my soul like he can see my private thoughts and dreams. I shiver.

New Boy smiles at me. I should smile back, cos a smile costs nothing and he must feel so alone, but I'm in a mood so I don't.

'Take that insolent look off your face,' says Mrs Partridge, turning her finger in a circle, indicating for me to face the wall. I am sure that's abuse. I swear I am going to phone ChildLine and report her.

So I turn round, but I can still feel New Boy's eyes on me. I try to distract myself by eavesdropping on Chrystal's poisonous whispers to Lily and Alba. But it's no good, I can still feel his eyes drilling into my bones.

I hear the bee humming again. I look at the reflection in the glass. New Boy holds out his hand and the bee just lands on his finger. I hold my breath and sneak a peek over my shoulder. He holds his finger close to his face and stares at the bee, then with the most gentlest movement, sends it on its way again – up, up, up into the rafters. I let out a loud gasp, my heart pounding a million beats a second.

New Boy turns round, looks straight at me and winks.

4

I quickly turn my face back against the wall –
I'm burning up. Then another thing happens.
The door beside me opens, just a bit, and a
brown eye and a pork-pie hat peep through it. I
reach out to open the door fully. It's Linford and
his wife Millie, no longer wearing their
tracksuits, looking fine and dapper in their
Sunday best.

'Naughty, naughty,' whispers Linford and
winks.

My shame burns me hotter at them seeing
me like this – in trouble, face against the wall.

'What are you doing at my school?' I hiss.

'You'll see,' whispers Millie, smiling.

Linford tweaks the end of my nose.

Great-Gran Beatrix had known him since he came over from Jamaica. It was my great-gran who introduced him to little silver-haired, twinkling Millie. It was Great-Gran Beatrix who bought him his pork-pie hat, as a thank you for saving my life when I was three and fell in that lake. She said it gave him dazzling style.

'But what are you doing here?' I whisper back.

'Shush,' snaps windbag Partridge, 'and who told you to turn around?'

I'm so surprised to see my friends in school that I just ignore her.

Mr Gregory spots Linford and Millie and beckons them on to the stage. 'I would like you all to welcome Millie and Linford, our special guests.' He claps his hands, so we all follow, applauding like polite little sheep as Linford struts past the gawping kids, Millie tottering behind.

Then the door opens again and in swishes Madame Bertha, in a long black skirt and turban, her black and gold cane tapping along the floor as she walks.

WHAT IS *SHE* DOING HERE?

Mr Gregory smiles. 'Madame Bertha, welcome.'

'Tut tut,' she says as she sees me in the corner.

I dig deep and give her my very best *I didn't want to do ballet anyway* face, and think my best *I have better things to occupy my time with, like bees and Judy and Marilyn films and my hat collection* thoughts.

Mrs Partridge waves her hand in the air for me to turn back round to the wall. I do as the old windbag says.

Then I hear Linford's voice ring out. 'In six weeks' time we will be having a very special Saturday in our village,' he announces. 'We are going to come together as a community to raise money for the Rise and Shine Happy Care Home for Older People. Ashton Junior School will join forces with Madame Bertha's Ballet and Tap Academy—'

Madame Bertha interrupts, 'Where, in the

evening, we will host a dance extravaganza. Many of you, such as Chrystal Kelly, attend my academy and will be performing.'

I hear excited whispers from girls and a few boys around me. Chrystal puffs out her chest and beams at the whole school.

'All the proceeds from the tickets will go to the Rise and Shine Home,' Madame Bertha booms.

'But,' says Linford, jumping back in, 'before the dance show there will be a sponsored swim. Millie and I are here to recruit volunteers from Ashton Junior School to take part.'

My belly sinks with an icy thud. *Water!* I shudder. I've only ever *swum* a width in my life. Well, not swum exactly, as I had arm floats on . . . I think back to how I struggled, splashing along to the rhythm of my class's clattering laughter.

I reach out to pull a dangle of peeling paint that's been tempting me from the wall.

'It's hard being old,' Linford continues.

My fingers freeze. I think about cuddling up

to Great-Gran Beatrix to watch *The Wizard of Oz* with a cup of tea and a sticky jam doughnut. The song 'Somewhere Over the Rainbow' whirls round and round in my head. She used to call me her little munchkin.

I can't help myself. I turn back round to face the stage as Linford's voice beats through the hall. He talks about the aches and pains and cold and loneliness of being old.

The old people in the Rise and Shine loved my great-gran and they love me, but all I do is lie, promising them that I will visit, saying, 'Tomorrow – I'll come tomorrow.' But tomorrow never ever comes.

I am a horrible person.

All my tomorrow-lies prickle in my belly. I decide there and then to change my ways. I tune into Linford again.

'The money raised will help buy warm food for old bellies and help pay for heating and blankets to warm old bones.'

I swallow his words. I pretend I can't see old windbag Partridge as she flaps her hands at me to turn to face the corner.

'Millie and I did a parachute jump last Saturday and raised three thousand pounds. My question is, will you help us raise another thousand?'

Chrystal turns round and mouths, 'Double-double-dare you.'

'I WILL!' I shout before I can stop myself.

'I will, I will, I will,' chants the rest of the school.

Chrystal mouths at me, 'You can't swim.'

I give her my best *I am not really scared of water, I am an Olympic swimming gold medallist* look.

'The sponsored swim will be held in six weeks' time at the leisure centre swimming pool,' says Linford. 'Followed by the dance extravaganza in Ashton Town Hall. The events will be opened by Mayor Kelly.'

Chrystal looks smug and turns back round to face the front. Lily and Alba nudge each other and giggle. Just cos her dad's mayor of Ashton, are we all meant to be impressed or something?

'The rules are, you have to be able to swim at least two lengths to enter,' says Millie, twinkling at us. 'So, any volunteers?'

Chrystal turns around again, laughs and shouts at me, 'You'll have to wear arm floats.'

Loads of hands go up in the air. 'Me, me, me,' they call.

And I can't help it – I stick my hand up and I lie. 'I can do it,' I say. 'I'll do the swim.'

Chrystal, who has obviously made a miraculous recovery from me knocking her on to the floor, jumps up and sticks her hand in the air as well.

Great-Gran Beatrix's words come to me. *'Bee, you have got to learn to swim. You can't let the waters get you.'*

'I promise you over the rainbow and back, Great-Gran Beatrix,' I'd said.

I shake my head so the words fall out of my ears. Because I hadn't kept my promise. I wanted to swim for her without my arm floats, but she died before I could learn how to do it.

The assembly hall is filling to the top with

'me, me, me's.

'QUIET,' yells Mr Gregory. 'One at a time.'

The hall falls silent and arms wave in the air like grass in the wind.

'Chrystal, let's start with you,' says Mrs Partridge, climbing up the steps to the stage and taking a pile of forms from Millie. 'Would you like to come up and get a sponsor form?' She turns to Linford. 'Chrystal's our champion swimmer,' she says.

Chrystal does this totally fake limp up to the stage to collect a sponsorship form. Madame Bertha rushes over to her in concern. Chrystal whispers in her ear and points at me.

I ignore them both, even though my cheeks are on fire, and kick my right DM heel back against the wall as Madame Bertha orders two Year Fives to help Chrystal back to her chair. Then more and more pupils from Years Four, Five and Six go up to collect their forms.

I feel like my ribs will bust from holding my hand in the air, but Mrs Partridge ignores me.

'Me, miss, me,' I say. 'PLEASE.'

Linford nudges Mrs Partridge and points in my direction. She ignores him too. Then New Boy snatches Timothy Lee's glasses from his nose and marches on to the stage. Quick as a flash, he reaches up and shoves the glasses on the end of Mrs Partridge's nose and points straight at me.

The whole school gasps. There is a deathly silence that seems to last for ever and the bee, still up in the rafters, sounds as loud as a drill. I'm biting my lip, trying not to laugh.

Mrs Partridge tears off the glasses.

'GO BACK TO YOUR SEAT!' she shouts at New Boy, her neck all blotchy and red.

'My office. NOW!' shouts Mr Gregory.

New Boy jumps off the edge of the stage, and strolls out of the hall as if he has all the hours and minutes in the world. Just as he reaches the door, Mrs Partridge calls out, 'Beatrix Daffodil Tulip Chrysanthemum Rose Edwards, why on earth is your hand up?'

'You can't swim two lengths,' Chrystal shouts out.

The whole school laughs. All except New Boy, who stops in his tracks.

'I can,' I say. 'Two lengths is easy.' It's my biggest lie yet.

Linford takes a form from Mrs Partridge and walks to the edge of the stage. I climb over people to get to him. Chrystal kicks me in the shin. As I reach for my sponsorship form, Linford whispers, 'Do it for your great-gran, munchkin. Make her proud.'

5

'I will see you in my office, Bee,' hisses Mr Gregory as the bell rings for the first lesson.

'You'd best tidy yourself up,' says Linford, reaching down to straighten my tie into a nifty knot.

'Go and look in the mirror,' Millie says, trying to brush down my shirt with her hand.

'I'll be cheering for you at the sponsored swim,' whispers Linford.

My gut helter-skelters to my toes. I clutch my sponsor form tight and elbow my way back to grab my school bag that someone has kicked out from under the assembly chair that I hardly sat on. Hauling my footprint-stamped bag on to my shoulder, I get carried along with the crowd, out of the door. Through the bobbing heads I see New Boy waiting outside the head teacher's office, hands in pockets, head bowed down.

Mrs Partridge is standing against the wall, scanning Year Six for untidiness as they walk past her. Like the best top-secret spy, I duck sideways into the girls' toilets before she sees me. I skid to the mirror and smack into the sink. Ow.

Propping my sponsor form against the taps, I start to patch up the mess made by Mrs Kelly's car and that muddy puddle. I wet my fingers and scrub at the dirt marks trickling down my cheeks and joining up my freckles into long brown lines.

I pull at my shirtsleeves to cover up the Biro bees I've drawn, flying up and down my arms. Tucking my shirt in and tugging my skirt straight, I glance down at my stripy socks. WHY, WHY, WHY hadn't I put on the regulation white ones today?

I pull off my mud-caked shoes and quickly run them under the tap, then hold them under the dryer for ten seconds. My lungs rattle. My chest tightens. The elephant returns to my chest. PANIC.

I tip my bag upside down and books, my bumblebee pencil case, a mirror and an old photo of Great-Gran Beatrix clatter over the tiles. But I can't see my inhaler anywhere. I shake out my PE trainer and the blue plastic inhaler bounces out. I grab it, breathe out, breathe in, inhale and hold for ten . . .

I breathe again. My lungs stop rattling. I have seen the elephant too many times already today. He does this as a warning sometimes – makes little visits before plonking himself on to my chest and staying put.

Throwing everything back into my bag, I race out of the door to the head teacher's office.

New Boy looks up and grins. I gasp – I've left my sponsor form on the taps. I race back and grab it, banging open the door as I leave and skidding back down the corridor. I trip over New Boy's feet as I try to stop outside Mr Gregory's office, and end up in a heap on the floor.

'Well, if it isn't Beatrix Daffodil Tulip Chrysanthemum Rose Edwards,' he says, grabbing my arm and pulling me up.

I dig into my scrapbook of expressions and give him my best *I am a stuntwoman and did that fall deliberately* face.

'Just call me Bee,' I gasp. 'Please.' My chest is still a little tight.

'Moon-Star Higgins,' he says, grinning, 'and whatcha looking at me like that for?'

'Moon-Star?' I repeat.

'Moon-Star's my name,' he mumbles.

'Oh,' I say and we grin at each other.

'We have wondrous names,' he says.

'Unusually strange,' I say. 'Beatrix Daffodil Tulip Chrysanthemum Rose Edwards and Moon-Star Higgins.'

'We are extraordinary,' he says, and suddenly I don't mind being called after a half-dead bunch of flowers from the petrol station. Those flowers have just started to bloom.

Then he grins at me again and I can't help but grin back, and it sparks into a smirk, then itches into a beam and explodes into the loudest laugh ever, till we are rolling on the floor, belly laughing.

'Beatrix Daffodil Tulip Chrysanthemum Rose Edwards and Moon-Star Higgins,' we shriek.

'GET UP OFF THE FLOOR NOW!'

Mrs Partridge is gliding towards us like the Wicked Witch of the West in *The Wizard of Oz*.

We haul ourselves to our feet and stand with our backs against the wall in silence as Partridge makes her witchy way down the corridor. I count the seconds till she's gone past, cos I am just dying to have a proper talk with Moon-Star. There are lots of questions I want to ask this strange new boy, who charms bees and has an extraordinary name. They joggle about in my brain but all that comes bursting out is, 'Thanks for not laughing at me in assembly about the swimming.'

Before Moon-Star can answer, Mr Gregory appears and does that head teacher thing, marching up and down the corridor and giving us the GLARE OF SILENT TORTURE every time he passes. The silence before the telling off is much, much worse than the words or any punishment.

Finally, when I think I can't bear it any longer, Mr Gregory stops in front of us.

'Go and wait in my office,' he almost-whispers.

We go in. Moon-Star stands next to me, hands in pockets, staring out of the window, and it's like he's not there. His thoughts are riding on the breeze.

Mr Gregory glares at us both.

It's my turn first. He puffs his face up like a red balloon and starts yelling without pausing for breath once.

'YOUR BEHAVIOUR IN ASSEMBLY WAS DISGRACEFUL DO YOU HEAR ME DISGRACEFUL PUSHING CHRYSTAL OFF THE CHAIR LIKE THAT WAS EXTREMELY DANGEROUS YOU MIGHT HAVE GIVEN HER A SERIOUS INJURY MISS WILLOW IS CHECKING CHRYSTAL'S LEG IN THE SICKBAY DON'T YOU REALISE SHE IS IN THE SCHOOL NETBALL TEAM SWIMMING TEAM ATHLETICS TEAM AND THE-END-OF-TERM DANCE GALA YOU WERE WRONG, VERY WRONG INDEED.'

As his face turns redder I concentrate on his

chins so I won't laugh. You know that thing where you laugh at something serious, even though you know you shouldn't? The cold starts to rise from your toes and the hairs on your arms stand on end, and before you know it you have this really stupid grin on your face and then you get yourself into even more trouble. But concentrating doesn't work, because as his chins wobble I feel this naughty giggle rising.

So I stand up really straight and concentrate instead on the patch of window I can see over Mr Gregory's right shoulder. Through it I see his rose garden.

'ARE YOU EVEN LISTENING TO ME, BEATRIX? YOU WERE WRONG—'

'But it's wrong to kill bees, sir,' I say before I can stop my mouth. 'I stopped Chrystal from murdering the honey-bee.' My voice cracks. 'Without bees pollinating the flowers you would not have your rose garden, sir. The bees are in terrible trouble and we need to save them.'

Mr Gregory's chins stop wobbling. He slumps like a flat tyre and sighs again.

'Well, Beatrix, you are right – I would not have my beautiful roses without the bees.'

Yes! I am saved. *Thank you, bees*, I say in my head.

But then he sees them. 'What are those stripy socks doing on your feet, Beatrix? It is rule seven in the Ashton Juniors rule book that "regulation white socks shall always be worn".'

'So people's eyes can see her,' mumbles Moon-Star.

'Speak PROPERLY,' bellows Mr Gregory.

'It's so she won't be invisible, sir,' repeats Moon-Star.

'What do you mean, invisible?' says Mr Gregory.

'Well, that lady with the long nose is obviously too blind to see that Bee had her hand up in the air for that swim thing. So I tried to help her out. If that lady can't see her then it's a smart thing that Bee does wear those stripy socks. Makes her stand out more.'

Mr Gregory's eyes goggle like a paralysed goldfish and his mouth drops open, but no more shouty words escape. He takes a big breath. His chins wobble faster.

'Let's start again, shall we? Moon-Star – welcome to Ashton Junior School. I hope you will be very happy with us. Beatrix will look after you, as you are in her class. Try not to lose him, Bee, like you lose everything else.' He laughs at his own very unfunny joke.

Moon-Star looks at me and raises his eyes to the ceiling.

Mr Gregory beckons us to sit in the two chairs in front of his desk. He reaches into a filing cabinet and brings out some forms. He hands them to Moon-Star with a pen.

'We ask all our new pupils to fill in these forms so we can learn a bit about you.'

'I'll do 'em later,' says Moon-Star, screwing them up in his hand.

'Now please,' insists Mr Gregory.

Moon-Star grips the pen with his fist like it's a hammer. He draws a moon and a star instead of writing his name.

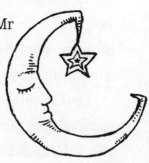

50

Tiny beads of sweat are appearing on his forehead. His hair seems to flatten against his scalp and all the life and sparkle trickles out of him. That's what happens to me in PE lessons.

And then the horrors kick me and I know in my gut that he can't write his name or read the forms. In PE lessons the ingredients that make me Bee vanish in a puff of smoke and I feel like Moon-Star looks at this very moment.

I know what it's like when you can't do something and people are watching you.

Mr Gregory coughs.

'If you can hurry up please, Moon-Star? I have a busy morning.'

I look at Mr Gregory with shock. IS HE BLIND? Can't he see what's happening to Moon-Star?

Dramatic action is called for. My mind ticks . . . Got it! This morning's literacy test. Perfect excuse!

I jump up.

'I forgot – we have a test!' I truth. 'Mrs Partridge told me in the corridor not to be

51

late,' I lie, cos I know full well Mrs Partridge would be quite happy for me to stay in the head teacher's office all day being shouted at. 'Please, Mr Gregory, Moon-Star and I have to go NOW. THIS SECOND. I promise I will make sure those forms get filled in and back to you.'

I grab Moon-Star's arm and the forms and pull him out of the room before Mr Gregory can speak.

We stand in the corridor. I am buzzing with cleverness at our escape. I grin at Moon-Star, but he just stares at me.

'I'll fill in the forms,' I say. 'Don't worry.'

The silence pounds, but the glint starts to trickle back into Moon-Star's deep-blue eyes.

'You shouldn't have done that. I CAN LOOK AFTER MYSELF,' he shouts, then he turns and scrambles through an open window. I watch as he sprints across the playing field, ducks under the gap in the hedge and vanishes.

6

I stare at the hedge that Moon-Star, my new might-have-been friend, disappeared beneath. What have I done? I only wanted to help. I will him to reappear, smile, tell me he was joking. I close my eyes, count to twenty and open them again, but there's nothing – just an empty playing field.

I drag my heavy heart back up the corridor to class. Why did I open my big, big mouth?

The door to the sickbay opens. I duck behind a pillar like a spy on a dangerous mission, then I peep round the side to see Chrystal limping out. I hold my breath. She looks around her but can't see me in my top-secret hiding place. Then she starts cartwheeling down the corridor. WHAT A FAKER. She stops opposite the cupboard with all the sports cups in it. The big silver one for Ashton Junior School Sports Girl of the Year, which she has won three years running, catches the light. She opens the cabinet, reaches for the cup and holds it high in the air, as if she is at the Olympics. I feel a naughty giggle rising and cram my fist in my mouth. She puts the cup back, then tap dances towards our classroom and slips inside. I breathe out and a snorty giggle escapes.

I tell myself that if I hop down the corridor, landing on all the squares of the tiles without touching any lines at all, then Moon-Star will appear.

I do it. He doesn't.

I open the door to the classroom. The test has already begun. Mrs Partridge puts her finger to her lips and hands me a worksheet.

'Is Moon-Star still with Mr Gregory?' she says, under her breath.

I nod a lie and shuffle into my seat, carefully and quietly. The chair scrapes against the floor.

'SHHHH,' spits Mrs Partridge.

I quickly shove Moon-Star's forms into my bag, hoping that old Partridge will think Moon-Star's with the head teacher and vice versa, so it will be a while before they catch on to his vanishing act.

Chrystal has laid out her set of pink gel pens next to her pink fluffy pencil case on her desk. Chrystal's desk is in the best place in the classroom, right by the window. I rifle through my bag for my stripy bumblebee pencil case. It's come open and all my pens have escaped to the bottom of my bag. I scramble to find one.

Mrs Partridge frowns at me. I grab a pen and start to go through the worksheet. As I slot all the commas, full stops and colons into place, my thoughts start to calm.

I look at the clock, watching as the second hand ticks round. Maybe Moon-Star will come back to school before the end of the day. I force my eyes back to the test and smile. It comes easy to me. I love the shapes the letters make, the way they dip and swerve and curl. I trace them with my finger, pretending I am a bee dipping in and out of flowers. I feel Mrs Partridge's eyes on me.

I finish the last question as slowly as possible. I want time to stop now cos I know what it's ticking towards . . .

PE.

But time doesn't stop. The second hand on the clock keeps tick, tick, ticking towards my doom.

A noise outside makes my head shoot up, but I'm disappointed to see that it's only the caretaker's ginger cat, Marmaduke, clattering against the shed tiles.

'Time's up,' says Mrs Partridge, collecting all the test papers. 'Hurry to the changing rooms for PE while the sun's still out.'

I take pigeon steps towards the changing rooms. 'Please rain,' I say over and over in my head. 'Please, please rain.'

I don't think people with top-secret spy potential should have to do PE. My mind flicks back to me emptying my bag for my inhaler. My heart stops.

My PE kit! It wasn't in there. Oh no! Mum told me to get it from the airing cupboard last night and I completely forgot. I'm going to get into so much trouble . . .

I dig into my virtual scrapbook for my best *I am far, far too ill to do PE and must be sent home immediately* face. Chrystal isn't the only faker round here.

'Beatrix,' sighs Mrs Partridge, 'stop pulling silly faces and get changed.'

'Pleeeease, Mrs Partridge, I don't feel well enough to do PE.'

'You weren't too ill to push Chrystal to the floor this morning. Nor were you too ill to volunteer for a sponsored swim!' she says, folding her arms and pulling a silly face herself. 'Forgotten our PE kit again, have we?'

She goes into her cupboard and pulls out the ancient smelly spares worn by pupils who forgot their PE kit a hundred years ago.

I scrunch up into the corner so that no one can see I still wear a vest when practically everyone else has a training bra.

I saw on *Film Stars – Fact or Fiction?* that Judy Garland was seventeen years old when she played Dorothy and they strapped her bumps down to make her look younger – that had to hurt loads! I expect she played with her little dog, Toto, between takes to make her feel better.

I would make a good Dorothy. I shut my eyes and dream that I am no longer clumsy Bee who was chucked out of Madame Bertha's Ballet and Tap Academy for not having a curtseying type of bottom, but I am Judy Garland, skipping down that yellow brick road to her destiny, with Toto and her friends – Tin Man, Lion and her favourite, Scarecrow – beside her.

'Stop daydreaming, Bee!' shouts Mrs Partridge.

I pull on a pair of baggy shorts that go right down to my knees and a top that is so short it shows off my freckly tummy. I try to pull it down, but it won't stretch. I smell disinfectant and feel itchy – they've most probably washed these clothes in toilet cleaner.

'Mrs Partridge wants me to collect

everybody's phones now,' shouts Chrystal. 'PUT YOUR PHONES IN THE BOX!'

Chrystal marches round being bossy phone monitor as usual, then she must remember that she is meant to have a life-threatening injury from when I pushed her this morning because she does a few fake limps.

She stops in front of me and smirks. 'Lovely PE kit, Bee. Have you put your phone in the box? Oh, whoops! I forgot! You haven't got one. The only girl in Year Six not to have a phone. How sad.'

'You don't need a phone, Chrystal,' I say. 'Just open your mouth – we can all hear you.'

'Hurry, hurry,' shouts Partridge, dragging a net of balls out to the playground. 'Get into pairs and practise your catching.'

Lily pushes me out of the way to grab Alba as her partner. Sarah, Ruth and Imogen all ignore me as they grab their own partners and the pushing, shoving boys all get into pairs. Eventually, I am the only one left, except for Timothy Lee who is standing there, blinking at me. I smile at him.

Mrs Partridge blows her stupid whistle.

Timothy throws me a ball. It stings my hand and I drop it.

He throws another one. It hits me on the side of the face, making my eyes water.

Chrystal laughs from a bench, where she is sitting because of her fake bad leg.

'Please can I get a drink of water, Mrs Partridge?' smarms Chrystal.

'Of course you can, Chrystal Saffron Kelly,' says Mrs Partridge, blowing her stupid whistle. 'Come on, everyone. One lap of the field! Let's see who wins now you haven't got Chrystal to beat you all.'

I run, all gangly legs and pointy elbows out of time.

Then I spot a blue thread dangling from a leaf on the hedge where Moon-Star disappeared. I grab it and hold it tight in my hand.

'Run,' I say to myself. 'Just run and get this over with.'

I come last. The elephant slowly takes its seat on my chest and I wheeze.

Mr Gregory is striding towards the field. Oh-no-no-no-no. He looks around. 'Where's Moon-Star?' he asks Mrs Partridge.

'Moon-Star . . .? Moon-Star!' The sniggers bounce around.

'Yep. He's got a unique, extraordinary, special name like me,' I puff. 'Get over it.'

Imogen grabs my elbow. 'Bee! Where's your inhaler?'

I nod towards the changing room.

Mr Gregory beckons me over. Oh-no-no-no.

'Please, sir,' says Imogen. 'Bee needs—'

'IN A MINUTE!' shouts Mr Gregory.

I walk towards him.

'Bee! What have you done with Moon-Star? You were meant to be looking after him.'

'Please, sir,' I puff. 'He's gone.'

'Sir,' says Imogen.

'Quiet,' says the head, and leads me away from the others.

'Couldn't you see,' I whisper-wheeze, 'couldn't you see that Moon-Star . . . can't read and write. You made him . . . so sad, sir, and I . . . tried to

help but . . . I just made it worse, like I always do.'
I open my hand and watch the blue thread dance
on the breeze and vanish like Moon-Star did. 'And
I—' I break off as an extra big wheeze escapes.

Imogen appears next to me and grabs my
elbow again.

'She needs her inhaler, sir. Please, it's in the
changing room.'

Mr Gregory's face goes oh-so red. 'Oh goodness
– yes of course! Imogen, go with Beatrix.'

Imogen takes my hand and gently leads me
over the field and into the changing room.

My bag lies on the floor, where I did not
leave it. I grab my inhaler, wheeze all the air
out of my lungs, breathe in, puff, hold for ten
and out. I repeat, giving myself a second dose.

Relief! I smile my thank-yous at Imogen. As
I put my inhaler back in my bag a piece of paper
flutters on to the floor. Imogen scoops it up and
hands it to me. It's my sponsor form, and along
the top a single word is scrawled in pink gel pen.

LOSER

7

'Oh, Bee,' says Imogen. 'This has to be reported to Mr Gregory.' She gently takes my sponsor form from me. 'Come on,' she says.

'No,' I say, snatching it back. 'It's fine. Please, don't say anything, Imogen, promise. You've got to promise me.'

Imogen stares at me for what seems like ages, then shrugs her shoulders. 'Let me take you to Miss Willow, at least. Maybe she'll send you home, what with you wheezing so badly.'

I wriggle out of the ancient, smelly PE kit and back into my school uniform.

As I follow Imogen down the corridor to Miss Willow's sickbay, I put on my best *I am really sick and should be sent home immediately* face.

I keep my fingers crossed – Miss Willow can be nice if she feels like it.

Miss Willow smiles when she sees me, sends Imogen on her way and leads me to the lovely big purple beanbags by the bookcase. She hands me a drink of water.

'You've not had an asthma attack for a while, have you, Bee?'

I nod my agreement.

'Is everything all right at home?' she asks.

Banging doors and heavy footsteps and shouts of '*How can you call your daughter after a half-dead bunch of flowers?*' rattle round my head, and suddenly I don't want to go home and I don't want to be at school and I don't want to be anywhere at all.

'Please,' I say, 'please, Miss Willow, can I have some quiet reading time?'

She smiles and I curl up in a ball, snuggling my black lambswool beret against my cheek, and I run my hand over the spine of the book I'm reading. I lose myself in dragons and castles and lands far away. Only it's Moon-Star slaying the dragon and climbing up the castle wall to rescue me. I turn redder than my hair. I shake my head so the thoughts will fall out of my ears and pick up a book on the French Resistance in the Second World War. Now I am Mademoiselle Le Bee in my beret – French super-spy, in a stylish stripy top, saving the world from war and . . .

I wake as gravel hits the window. I jump up, thinking it might be Moon-Star, but I hear girls giggling and footsteps running away.

I look at the clock. It's 3.45 p.m. I've missed lunch. I've been asleep for hours!

'I nearly forgot about you,' laughs Miss Willow, poking her head round the door. 'Time to go home. Are you feeling better?'

I nod a lie as I put on my beret and sling my bag over my shoulder.

I'm last through the school gates as usual. Imogen sits on the wall, head buried in a book, chewing the end of a pencil. Her mum drives up in a silver car and parps her horn. Imogen jumps up and scurries to the car.

'Bye, Imogen,' I call. But she doesn't hear me. The silver car hums as it moves away, and now the road is empty.

I ponder my problems and make a worry list in my head:

Worry number 1: Moon-Star Higgins – potential new friend made and lost in a day!

Problem: I have a big mouth.

A bee flies just in front of my nose, landing on a patch of daisies by the roadside. I watch it fly from flower to flower.

Worry number 2: the bees are in danger and if we have no bees pollinating then we will have no vegetables or fruits or flowers and the world will be black and white like in the old films and we will all die horribly from having no vitamins.

Problem: No one else seems to care about this. Except for Moon-Star the bee charmer.

Worry number 3: One sponsored swim entered.

Problem: No swimming skills whatsoever. PLUS I AM SCARED OF WATER.

The bee finishes its work and flies off into the warm breeze which tickles my face and makes my school skirt flutter and I am no longer worried Bee with gangly legs, clumpy boots and pointy elbows. Instead I am film star Marilyn Monroe with dainty high heels and white swirly skirts that dance in the wind as it swishes them around. I do Marilyn's wiggly-waggly walk and suddenly I have rhythm; I am a star.

Until I hear a noise.

'Is anybody there?' I shout and look around. Nothing.

I count to three before I carry on walking.

The late afternoon sun dazzles my eyes and makes the road ahead yellow.

Now I am Judy Garland playing Dorothy, only there is no Tin Man, no Lion and no Scarecrow. But I carry on walking down that yellow brick road anyway.

I am quite alone. Or am I?

I hear a footstep behind me. I turn. Still nothing. I continue to walk – but slower this time. A stifled snort. I turn and my voice shakes out, 'Who's there?'

Chrystal steps out from behind a tree, poison

in her eyes. Then, one by one, girls from my class appear out of doorways, from behind benches and bushes, and walk towards me, mocking my wiggly-waggly walk. My rhythm and swirly skirts vanish. I am just Bee again with gangly legs in clumpy boots.

I run towards the woods, hoping the trees will hide me, but Chrystal overtakes me and blocks my way. Lily and Alba grab my arms, pinching my skin. My beret is ripped from my head.

Chrystal holds it high in the air.

'My hat! Give it back!' I scream, launching myself at her, but hands grab me and start pushing and shoving me. The elephant begins to lower itself on to my chest and I find myself sinking down, down, down, and I can't breathe.

I reach for my inhaler but my bag is kicked away. 'Please,' I whisper. I shut my eyes and see Great-Gran Beatrix reaching out to me. I'm gasping for breath . . .

Then a pounding rhythm on the ground beneath me beats into my body, there's yelling – scream upon screech upon scream, and their

68

hands let me go.

A warm nose breathes hot sweet air on my face. I open my eyes and find I am staring into the eyes of the most ginormous brown and white horse. Arms grab me tight and heave me up into the air and on to the horse's back.

IT'S MOON-STAR!

He jumps up on to the horse behind me and puts his arms around my waist. I feel the horse's body rippling with strength beneath my shaking legs. My wheezes are getting louder.

'Grab on to his mane.' Moon-Star places my hands on the horse's hair; it feels warm and coarse between my fingers. 'And wrap your legs round his belly,' he whispers in my ear as we ride away.

The smooth, steady rhythm of the horse's movements pulses through me. Twigs catch my hair and scratch my arms as we break into a gallop through the trees towards—

No – it can't be.

'Stop,' I whimper. 'STOP! We're going towards Old Alice's wagon . . . PLEASE, STOP!' But all that comes out is a stream of panicky wheezes.

The horse slows down and begins prancing round in a circle, snorting. I lose my grip and start to topple off his back.

A pair of gnarled hands grab me and Old Alice's face is up in mine, pushing my hair out of my eyes.

'Meet my gran,' says Moon-Star.

8

'Get the girl inside.'

'No!' I scream, but all that hits the air is another wheeze.

I will myself to struggle, but my legs flop. The elephant is winning. I shut my eyes tight as tight can be.

Moon-Star carries me inside, and my back bounces against a soft mattress. I feel Old Alice's rough hands around my face.

'Look at me, child,' she says. 'Where's your puffer for the wheezes?'

I count – one, two, three – and open my eyes. I look into Old Alice's, deep blue and staring into my soul.

'You had a bag with you this morning, when

you ran from me. Is your puffer inside it?'

I nod.

'Some screeching girls were chasing her, Gran. They had her cornered like a caught animal,' says Moon-Star.

'Moon-Star, ride back, see if you can find it. Hurry,' Old Alice says.

'Moon-Star!' I wheeze, but he's gone, leaving me alone with the witch.

'Old Alice will see you right, girl,' she says as she props my head up on a pillow stuffed with lavender. My wheezes rattle as she heats some water and mixes it with honey. 'The bees will help you,' she says and hands me a scratchy pottery tankard.

I try to smile as I sip but I am sure it looks weak and pathetic.

As the honey trickles down my throat the elephant shuffles a bit.

'I didn't . . . know,' I puff, 'that honey . . . helps asthma.'

'Oh ay,' says Old Alice. ''Tis the secret of the bees.'

My grey cardigan is folded up on the end of the bed. There is an open window beside the bed with golden curtains that glisten in the sunlight. I reach out and stroke them.

'Made 'em myself with my own hands,' says Old Alice.

I look around, but there are no cobwebs or witchy cauldrons like in my nightmares. Instead, I'm in the most bewitchingly beautiful place I have ever seen.

It's red and gold and bronze and copper, everywhere. Along one side of the wagon is a mini cooker with bronze pots and pans boiling on the hob. There are little cupboards with small shelves above them, displaying jar upon jar of honey and bottles of herbs and spices.

Along the other side is a red sofa with golden cushions and, beside it, a table and two chairs. There is a bronze lamp in every corner.

The door of the wagon is like a stable door, split in half so that you can open up the top or bottom. The top half is open and through it I can see trees swaying in the breeze.

I lift my finger to trace the gold swirls and swishes stitched into the red velvet cover I am lying on and I get this feeling I would be happy to stay here for ever.

Old Alice switches on a copper contraption on the cooker, and a warm, gentle steam fills the air. I start to relax.

She leans over me. 'Don't mind me,' she says and she reaches for a button of my shirt. I shrink away. 'Oh, vest-shy are we? You've nothing I haven't seen before. You'll be a woman soon enough, and we need to get you breathing so you can be a strong one.'

I let her undo the buttons and she lays her rough, gnarled hands on my lungs. I feel the heat from her palms. And as my lungs start to breathe, Old Alice closes her eyes and mutters what sounds like the names of herbs and spices. Then she covers me with a blanket and starts to reach for the bottles on the little shelves. I watch as she starts to chop their contents, muttering all the time. A strange calmness washes over me. She's charmed me like she does the bees.

Old Alice pulls back the blanket, puts a muslin cloth on my flat chest and spoons a mushy pulp on top. I fight sleep.

I wake to the sound of purring. It's the little grey kitten, lying on my chest, blinking at me with his wide green eyes.

'I tried to move him,' says Old Alice, 'but he's a wandering soul and just came right back here. He knows you're ill – he's not left your side. Your breathing didn't worsen, so it don't look like you're allergic to cats, eh?'

I think back to the allergy tests I had done on my arm at the hospital when I was seven. The cat one had not come up as a red itchy lump like some of the others had.

'No, just budgies, dust, guinea pigs . . .'

'I daresay you're allergic to the upsets, too,' she says, giving me a wink.

The little kitten's purrs vibrate through my lungs, making them come to life.

I stretch out my arm to stroke him. He licks

my finger with his teeny tiny tongue.

'Thinks you need a bath,' laughs Old Alice and she brings a bowl of warm water and a flannel over to the bed.

I look down at my scuffed knees from where I hit the ground. She gently bathes them and pours honey on them.

'It's manuka honey – has special healing powers,' she says.

Then Old Alice picks up my arms and looks at my Biro bee tattoos and shakes her head, chuckling to herself.

The sound of horse hooves approaching come from outside the wagon. The door opens. Moon-Star runs in with my bag.

He tips it upside down, and books, my bee pencil case, bumblebee mirror, Moon-Star's forms, the photo of Great-Gran Beatrix, and lastly my inhaler bounce on to the bed. The kitten bats it with his paw. I grab it, breathe out, breathe in, puff and hold for ten and out. The last of the wheezes go.

Moon-Star pulls a dirty blob of black material

out of his pocket. It's my precious beret.

'This yours? Found it stamped all over.'

I nod, angry when a tear escapes. I flick it away.

Old Alice takes it from Moon-Star.

'We'll have it bright and new.'

She holds it next to her steamer, and the dirt starts to slide off. She gently reshapes it. I blink another tear away at her kindness.

She hands it back to me and I sit up and wriggle my head into it. Great-Gran Beatrix always said it was one of her favourites out of all the hats she ever gave me. She said that with my red hair and black beret I looked unique and distinctive – one of a kind.

I feel so awkward about what happened this morning when I ran away from Old Alice. To make myself busy, I look at my books and pencil case and smooth out the photo. Great-Gran Beatrix's eyes twinkle up at me.

MY SPONSOR FORM! Where is my sponsor form?

The kitten hisses as my mood changes.

He jumps down and hides behind a pile of books.

'Oh, Bob, no!' says Moon-Star.

I turn to see that the horse has put his nose through the open window and has something white dangling from his mouth. It's my sponsor form!

Moon-Star grabs Bob's jaw and gently prises the form from his mouth. He hands the crinkled soggy mess to me.

The kitten pounces and bats Bob on his nose. Bob snorts and jumps back.

'I apologise for Bob's manners,' Moon-Star says. 'He chews everything. Not never met a beast like him for sure. Ate a fifty-pound note once. He don't seem to learn oats is food, paper is not.'

I smooth out the crinkled mess. One of the corners is tattered. The pink ink at the top is now just a splodge. I start to laugh.

'Least I can't read "loser" any more,' I say.

9

'Who wrote that? You ain't no loser,' says Moon-Star, grinning at me.

My heart lightens.

'Bendy tap-dancing freak,' I say. 'I know it was her for sure.'

'Who?' says Old Alice.

'Bendy tap—' The daggers in her eyes make me stop.

'Who?' says Old Alice.

'Chrystal Kelly,' I say.

'That's better,' says Old Alice. 'We use proper names, not nicknames out of spite in this home.'

'Is Chrystal that girl who got stung on the hand and screamed so loud she scared the bees and the birds from the trees?' says Old Alice.

'Yes,' I say. 'She used to be my best friend.'

'Talking of names, what be yours?'

'Beatrix Daffodil Tulip Chrysanthemum Rose Edwards. Just call me Bee. Please, please call me that.'

'Your flower names are fine names – you should be proud. But if your wish is for me to call you Bee, then Bee 'tis.'

After a while she says, 'And this Chrystal one, were it her who chased you?'

I nod. There's no use lying to Old Alice. I think she would just know if I was.

'Why does she chase you so?' asks Old Alice.

'Because I'm different,' I say and I can feel my chin jutting out. It's what Great-Gran Beatrix called my stubborn face.

'Different is good,' she says and our eyes lock in understanding.

She starts stirring something in a pot on the stove. 'Well, Bee, you will stay and eat, won't you? What's ours is yours. You are most welcome.'

'BOB!' cries Moon-Star. I turn. The horse has the golden curtain in his mouth.

Old Alice leaps across the wagon to the window and pushes the horse back by his nose.

'Moon-Star Pluto Higgins, will you get that beast's nose out of here. Go and give Bob his tea. Make yourself useful.'

'Pluto,' I snort. 'You never told me that this morning.'

'Didn't choose to,' sniffs Moon-Star as he saunters out after Bob. 'Ain't your business.'

He's a moody one to be sure, I think.

'He's moody Moon-Star,' I say to the grey kitten, who is now curled up on my legs, asleep. Old Alice laughs.

And then all at once there is a clatter. The black and grey cat leaps down from the top of a cupboard, grabs her sleeping kitten by its scruff and vanishes.

'That cat be a good ratter – the best we got,' Old Alice says. 'Keeps us vermin-free. Maybe now all the beasts have gone, we can eat some vittles in peace! Do you think you're strong enough to wash your hands? There's a tap outside.'

I nod. I know I should be going home. My mum and dad will be wondering where I am, but I just can't seem to leave this place. Funny how it once brought screams and it now brings laughter and joy.

I swing my legs from the bed and wriggle into my school cardigan. It seems years ago now that I ran away from her, leaving my cardigan behind. I feel a bit shaky as I walk to the door and down the five steps to the ground.

Bob's nose is in a bucket, slurping water over the sides, then he lifts his head and munches on a pile of hay next to it. Moon-Star stands next to him, patting the horse's long brown neck. He looks up at me and grins. Ignoring him, I walk over to the rusty old tap and turn it on, letting the cold water splash between my fingers. I want to speak to Moon-Star, but I feel all elbows and knees – awkward, stupid, shy. I sneak a peek; he is still looking at me and grinning. He beckons me over.

'Ever befriended an 'orse before?' he says.

I shake my head. 'They're a bit big,' I say, 'but so beautiful. I've dreamed of riding horses before but never ever done it . . . till today!' I pause. 'Thanks, for rescuing me,' I mutter and I flash him my best *thanks for rescuing me but I am an amazing stuntwoman and can actually rescue myself* face.

'Whatcha screwing up your face for, Bee? Come and say hello to Bob properly.'

Bob takes his nose out of the bucket. I put out my hand but he goes to nibble my fingers. I jump back.

'Like this,' says Moon-Star, grabbing my hand and placing it on Bob's brown-with-white-patches coat. We stroke him, our fingers muddled as one. The horse feels nice – soft and warm.

'I like the white diamond shape above his eyes,' I say.

''Tis called a star by horse people – that's why we belong together. Moon-Star and Bob the gypsy cob.'

'Bob the cob,' I giggle. 'He's got a very long fringe. And hairy feet.'

Moon-Star laughs. ''Tis called a forelock, not a fringe, and the hairy feet are called feathers. Bought Bob from Appleby Fair from a Romany boy I know – Joe's his name. Romanies leave the forelock as nature intended. It's good cos it keeps the flies out of Bob's eyes.'

My fingers are still muddled with Moon-Star's as we stroke Bob. They feel tingly.

'Bee, 'bout today and me not being in school. Gran mustn't—'

Moon-Star rips his hand away like I've scalded him. Old Alice is standing behind us.

'Moon-Star and Bee, wash your hands now. Vittles are ready . . .' And she shows us over to the tap and up the stairs to the wagon where a scrummy feast waits for us on the table.

'Sit yourself down,' she says, pointing to a chair.

Old Alice takes the other one and Moon-Star brings a wooden box from outside and perches on it. Laid out on the table are bowls and dishes painted with wondrous pictures of horses and bees and flowers and bushes and trees, and others with princesses and unicorns and strange exotic beasts.

Old Alice dishes up yummy leek and potato soup and passes around hunks of homemade bread dripping with honey from the bees. I can't stop eating. I eat and eat and eat, as if it's my last meal.

'I guess today's commotions have made your belly hollow,' laughs Old Alice, cutting me a slice of gooey chocolate cake.

I nod as I take a mouthful. Oh! It melts in my mouth.

'I should explain, Bee,' says Old Alice. 'When you ran from me this morning, I was just trying to tell you that my grandson was coming to your school.'

'I am truly sorry,' I say. 'I was stupid. You made me jump and I—'

'Never mind all that now – what I need to know is how Moon-Star did today at school. Did he pick up a pen and do book learning or did he get the jitters in his feet?'

'Gran!' says Moon-Star.

'Hush, let the girl answer. I've heard too many of your fairy tales over the years.'

I feel Moon-Star's eyes drilling into my bones.

'He did pick up a pen,' I truth. I don't say that he threw it down and vanished for the rest of the day.

Old Alice gets up and walks over to the bed. 'Well, Bee, you seem to have a lot of books and papers and whatnot.'

She picks up a book and the papers and turns around. 'Moon-Star Higgins, where are all your books and papers? Didn't that school give you nothing?'

'These are Moon-Star's,' I say quickly, standing up and taking the papers from her. 'He dropped them most probably without realising, so I rescued them. I promised Mr Gregory, the head teacher, that he would fill them in for tomorrow. I'm meant to be looking after him but I don't think I did a very good job.

I'm so sorry.'

'Don't need no looking after,' growls Moon-Star, and the wooden box goes flying as he makes for the wagon door.

'COME BACK HERE NOW. THIS IS YOUR LAST CHANCE, MOON-STAR!' booms Old Alice, loud enough to make the walls shake.

I am curious about what she means by 'last chance'.

Slowly Moon-Star turns and slumps back on the wooden box.

'Now then, Bee,' says Old Alice. 'We'd both be grateful if you could help us with those there forms. I've never been one for the book learning myself. Keep it all in my head, see, but times are changing and Moon-Star's got to learn his letters. Or . . . well, let's say the consequences will be catastrophic.'

I go to the bed and select my best fluorescent green pen out of my bumblebee pencil case, then remember they are Moon-Star's forms not mine and swap it for a boring old Biro. Mr Gregory is not a fan of fluorescent pens. Neither is windbag Partridge, who has given me several detentions because fluorescent pens are NOT SUITABLE for use in homework. Anyway, I must not be selfish, but a responsible, helpful person, who does not lose people they have been told to look after, and helps people fill in boring forms with boring Biros.

As I turn back to the table, I dig into my virtual scrapbook of expressions for my best *I am a kind person who will not lose you and will help you fill in your forms* face.

'Are you feeling ill again, child? It takes time to recover from an attack of the wheezes.'

'No, I'm fine,' I say, cos I am. Old Alice is a miracle worker.

I smooth out the papers on the table and fill in Moon-Star's name. I leave the question about previous schools blank. I have a feeling it's probably best not to go into that.

'It asks if you have any allergies?' I say.

'Yep,' says Moon-Star. 'I'm allergic to schools and teachers and desks, and being shut in, and being bossed around by girls, and books and reading and writing. How's that for starters?'

Fire lights in my belly. I have had enough of his moods. I'm only trying to help. 'I'll be going then,' I say, 'cos I don't have to do this for you. I've got better things I could be doing.'

As I stand up, the table wobbles.

'MOON-STAR,' growls Old Alice. 'Bee, we are most grateful to you.'

I slowly sit down again and pick up the pen, giving him my best *you are so lucky that I am even talking to you, Moon-Star Higgins* face.

'Moon-Star ain't allergic to nothing,' says Old Alice.

Next question. I read, 'What things do you like to do?'

There's a sulky silence from Moon-Star.

'Go on, answer the girl,' says Old Alice, digging him in the shoulder.

Moon-Star sighs, stares into the distance and slowly, slowly, his face lights up. 'I like riding Bob in the early morning when the dew hits the grass,' he says. 'Then when Bob lies down for a nap, I curls up with him and rest my head on his belly and we dream of riding along the beach, through the splashing waves. I like running among the trees and listening to the birds and making whistles out of sticks and watching the rabbits play and warning them when the cats are near. I like holding the kittens that Gran has here in her feral colony and tickling their little tummies. I like being wild and free and not trapped in a classroom.'

His face slumps as he finishes speaking. I scribble down his words and wish I were riding through the waves with him, even though I HATE WATER. What is wrong with me?

'What is your favourite subject?' I read.

'None, hate school,' growls Moon-Star.

'Moon-Star likes painting and drawing – he did all these,' says Old Alice, picking up the bowls.

My jaw hits my belly button. 'You did these? They are the most beautiful things I have ever seen – good enough for film stars to eat off.'

'Is this Moon-Star's?' says Old Alice, picking up my sponsor form.

'No.' My stomach does a flip-flop. 'It's mine, but I wish with my whole heart it wasn't. I shouldn't have stuck my hand in the air for the sponsored swim cos I'm scared of water and I told my great-gran I'd learn to swim and I can't . . . I just can't.'

Moon-Star and Old Alice gape at my outburst and the silence seems to stretch on and on.

'You can,' says Old Alice eventually, 'and you will. I'll sponsor you a pound a length.'

She grabs the Biro and draws an X on the form. 'The cross is my bond.'

She looks from me to Moon-Star, then back to me again.

'Now, seems to me, Moon-Star and Bee, that you need to make a travellers' pact.'

I look at Moon-Star. He sits very still and I hold my breath. Then he nods very, very slowly.

'A travellers' pact it is then, Gran.'

10

'Outside,' says Moon–Star.

'Aye,' says Old Alice. 'This travellers' pact must be sworn on in secret, so that only the two of you shall know its words.'

I feel excited, even though I don't know what they're talking about. I follow Moon–Star down the wagon steps and catch up with him as he walks along, his hands in his pockets and whistling a haunting tune.

After a while I say, 'What's a travellers' pact?'

He totally ignores me, picks a tall blade of grass and chews it, then after what seems like for ever, he spits it out and says, 'It's swapping things.'

'Oh, swapping things,' I say, trying to find

my best *I am super-intelligent and understand totally what you are talking about, even though I have no clue* face.

We go down the pathway, through the long grass and trees, towards the beehives. My heart starts thudding. We tread softly through the swarms of whirring honeybees dancing circles round my hair, until Moon-Star suddenly stops at the Promise Tree, turns and grabs my arm hard. Like the first time I saw him, his blue eyes pierce through me and it feels as if he can see my private thoughts and dreams. I shiver.

'Bee, 'bout what Gran said . . .' Moon-Star kicks at a tuft of grass by his foot. Then he mumbles the next words so quickly I can hardly hear them. 'Need your help with the reading and writing letters.'

My toes tingle with pride.

'Of course I'll help, Moon-Star, but you'll learn in school too. Mrs Partridge will . . .'

'No, it's gotta be you, Bee. Schools, see, they make me feel trapped, like the walls are closing in, squeezing the breath out of me.'

'But you've got to go to Ashton Juniors,' I say. 'Everyone has to go to school.'

Moon-Star looks so miserable my heart aches.

'I know I got to go. I'm on my last chance,' he says quietly.

'I don't understand,' I say. 'Last chance for what? You must have been to school in the last place you lived?'

'No, cos I been living with Daisy – that's my ma.'

'Isn't there a school where your ma lives?' I ask, confused.

'You don't get it. Me and Ma, we travel around in the Daisymobile – that's our camper van what I painted daisies on special for her birthday.'

I conjure up an image of a beautiful camper van covered in flowers, never having to go to school, exploring villages and towns – total freedom, like honeybees that can fly wherever they want to.

'Where's your ma now?'

Moon-Star gets this faraway look in his eyes. 'Daisy runs through fields, with her hair wild in the wind and bells on her toes and she dances by the campfire all night and laughs so loud

I swear the flames of the fire flicker.'

'Your mum sounds so beautiful and free,' I whisper.

'She's free as the wind,' says Moon-Star.

'Free as a bird,' I laugh.

Moon-Star nods. 'There ain't no one like her. She taught me how to make the call of the birds, so they sing back to you. She taught me to make dens and whistles out of sticks, but she never taught me no letters. And then this busybody came and said I had to go to school at a special place where boys sleep and learn reading and writing.'

'What did you do?' I ask, holding my breath.

'So we left in the Daisymobile in the dead of night and went to the next village. But the busybodies, they kept coming. Till Gran came a-calling and said to my ma, "Daisy, enough! Do you want them to take Moon-Star away from you? The boy comes home with me and goes to school to learn proper reading and writing." And so I did, and I'm here and I needs your help, Bee.'

My pride explodes into a huge smile. 'I'll be your teacher,' I say.

Moon-Star smiles back. 'You better not be too bossy.'

I shake my hair and dig into my scrapbook for my best *I am an excellent teacher* face.

'And *I'll* teach you to swim – that's the swap, see? That's the Higgins travellers' pact that can't be broken.'

I feel my smile freeze. I try to swallow. 'What?' I say.

'You heard me. I'm going to get you swimming for that sponsored swim thing.'

'But I can't,' I say. 'The waters will get me. I just can't.'

And then there's a rustling in the trees and the bees are murmuring and I swear it sounds like Great-Gran Beatrix whispering, 'Learn to swim for me, munchkin. Do it for your Great-Gran Beatrix.'

I nod my head because no words will come.

'Is that a yes?' says Moon-Star. 'Cos you gotta say it out loud otherwise the pact don't count.'

'Yes,' I whisper.

'Vow on the Promise Tree,' he says, placing

my hand on the ancient words carved into the oak. Words that I've heard about but never ever seen, with it being so close to Old Alice's wagon and me being foolish and afraid.

'Read them words to me,' says Moon-Star.

Some of the words are grown over with moss, some are so faint that I have to squint my eyes, but I read and read and read.

Behold the ancient pact of the town of Ashton. In the reign of King James, a bond was made betwixt the mayor of Ashton and those who travel betwixt dell and dale, on the day the mayor's beloved baby daughter, Elizabeth, was saved from the waters by the travellers. From this day forth, travelling folk shall be free to rest in the clearing by the hives in the wood and shall live in peace and harmony with the bees and nature.

Should this bond be broken, the bees will swarm and all the flowers and crops shall perish.

I gasp. 'The waters, they tried to get a baby

– that poor little girl.'

'The waters shan't get you,' says Moon-Star. 'I'll keep you safe. Now, do you swear on the bees that you will teach Moon-Star Higgins his letters?'

'I do,' I say. 'I swear on the bees to teach you to read.'

'In return, I, Moon-Star Higgins, promise to teach you to swim through the waters and keep you safe.'

He presses my hand hard against the oak and whispers the words I have to say next into my ear. Then we say as one, 'The Promise Tree shall keep the Higgins travellers' pact.'

'You first,' I say, and we run round the oak tree, tracing the letters of promises carved into the bark with our fingers.

'Look,' I read. '*I, Arthur Jones, promise to marry Amy Jackson when the war is over. 1 September 1939.*'

An idea suddenly pops into my head as I look at the deep dips and curves of the letters carved into the tree.

'Don't you see, Moon-Star? The letters that make up the words of the promises, they are just shapes, like you see in nature. Shapes like you painted on your cups and plates.'

I take his finger and trace the letters.

'Look, a "v" – that's just like the shape of a valley. I bet you drove into valleys in the Daisymobile with your mum. And look, this is an "n" – it's the shape of a hill. Imagine riding Bob to the top of the hill and looking down at all the tiny people and houses below.'

Moon-Star's lip twitches. He almost smiles.

'"A" is for "Amy". That's your first letter.' And we make the shape with sticks from the Promise Tree.

'Then comes the most important letter and don't you forget it,' I say.

'What's that then?' says Moon-Star.

'B, of course! It is the most extraordinary, amazing letter in the alphabet.'

Moon-Star shoves me and laughs, pulling me down so that I'm sitting next to him in the long grass. We squint at the bees as they fly in circles above us, and we trace the shape of a letter 'B' with our fingers. Then I pull him up and we creep past the bees and run laughing in the curve of a letter 'C', through the grass and back to the Promise Tree.

A loud, frightened whinny cuts the air, followed by the thunder of horse hooves. Bob gallops down the path, then rears when he comes to the hives. The bees are angry, their hum swelling to a loud crescendo. Bob squeals then gives a snort.

'Whoa, boy, whoa,' says Moon-Star, walking slowly through the bees, his arms outstretched, till he reaches Bob and, with tender sweetness, strokes his nose. Then Moon-Star turns and walks back to join me under the branches of the Promise Tree. Bob follows him like a baby lamb.

'Something made you afraid,' whispers Moon-Star. 'What is it, Bob? What's scared you, boy?'

Then I hear them – men's voices, crashing through the trees. I know those voices. They belong to Alfie and Burt, Mayor Kelly's stooges.

Moon-Star puts his fingers to his lips and I bury my face in Bob's neck, breathing in his comforting sweet horsey smell. We keep really still.

'Ain't right,' says Alfie. 'The old woman and that brat she's got staying with her should be moved on.'

'Yep,' says Burt. 'Mayor's got plans. Wants to build houses in the clearing. We got to get rid of the old lady, make her move on. She's not wanted round here.'

I am like a spy hidden in the woods, but I don't like it this time. It isn't make-believe. It's real, and it feels as if we are in danger.

The voices move on past us and disappear into the distance.

Slowly I lift my face up from Bob's neck and look at Moon-Star.

A single tear trickles down his cheek.

11

Moon-Star turns and buries his face in Bob's mane. I guess he doesn't want me to see he's crying. I reach out slowly and put my hand on his shoulder but he shrugs it off.

'Those men . . .' My voice trails off because for once in my whole life I have run out of words.

'Don't worry about it,' he hisses, 'we're used to it – happens all the time to us travellers. Go on, Bee, go back to your . . .' He pauses and spits out, '*House.*'

Dusk has fallen to dark; the bees are sleeping. I look up at the twinkly night sky, and I know that the brightest star of all is Great-Gran Beatrix looking down at me and smiling. She would want me to be kind to Moon-Star, even though he's spitting anger.

'Will you be at school tomorrow, Moon-Star?' I ask.

He shrugs his shoulders.

'Remember the pact,' I say. 'You don't want them to send you away.'

He shrugs his shoulders again and keeps his back to me.

I stand there like an idiot, count to twenty and say, 'I'm going then – good night, Moon-Star, sleep tight, Bob.' I whisper good night to the sleeping bees and run up the path away from the Promise Tree, elbows and knees joggling as usual.

Old Alice is sitting on the steps of the wagon, smoking a pipe. The scent of tobacco wafts through the air and makes my nostrils flare with the smell of mysteries and ancient times.

'Made your pact?' she mutters.

'Yes, on the Promise Tree,' I say.

'Oh ay,' she says, nodding.

'Bye,' I call and wave. It's on the tip of my tongue to tell her about Burt and Alfie's hurtful words, but all that comes out is, 'Thank you so much for the lovely tea.' It's not my business to tell Old Alice – Moon-Star should.

I joggle a few more steps, then it hits me with a hammer. MY BAG!

I turn. Old Alice is chuckling as she holds my bag in the air. 'Forgotten something, child? I've packed it up for you.'

I walk back to the wagon steps, grinning. 'I forget things all the time,' I say.

'You'll not forget who your friends are, I hope,' she says, chucking me under the chin. Old Alice puts her hand over her pipe to put it out and jumps up. 'I'll walk you through the wood. I like to pick mushrooms in the cool of the night.'

We walk in silence through the clearing, along to the road, between the trees, lost in thoughts. There are no birds singing, no cars, just Old Alice's skirts bustling.

As we near the bridge I hear the swirling waters getting closer, calling me to them.

I dig deep and hard for my best *I am totally cool with walking over the bridge* face.

'I'll be OK from here, Old Alice, honestly.'

I don't want to do my twenty-five hops over the bridge in front of her.

Alice stares at me for what seems for ever and I hold my breath. 'Get home now, and don't you be running. Walk – give your lungs a chance to heal. Here,' she says, reaching into her pocket. She presses a little muslin bag into my hand. 'Put that under your pillow; it'll help you sleep.'

I slip it into my pocket and watch her bustle off through the trees, stooping every now and again to pick mushrooms. Then, just as I am about to turn and do my first hop she hollers through the trees, 'Remember, the pact can never be broken!'

'Broken, broken, broken . . .' echoes through the branches, then she's gone.

I swallow, turn, and see the waters taunting me. I take a deep breath and start to hop on my right foot.

1, 2 – what am I doing? 3, 4, 5 – I can't learn to swim! 6, 7 – I'm rubbish at everything – 8, 9, 10, 11 – everyone will just laugh at me as usual – 12, 13 – I'm never ever, ever, ever going to be able to do this sponsored swim – 14, 15, 16, 17 – I'll drown! 18, 19 – why oh why oh why did I make the pact with Moon-Star?

I wobble and lurch into the railing at the side of the crooked bridge, my face thrown towards the waters. I feel myself being sucked under, down, down, down . . . Then I hear in my head, '*Do it for me, munchkin.*' I force my arms out and somehow manage to stand straight without putting my left foot on the floor and I hop and hop and hop – 20, 21, 22, 23, 24. And one big huge long hop – 25!

I'VE DONE IT! I should be in the Olympics as a champion hopper. I hold my head high and I smile my film-star smile at my adoring fans.

By now, it's grown dark and I need to get home. There's no place like home, after all. I speed up and now I am Judy being Dorothy, skipping down the yellow brick road with determination. I will learn to swim. I can do anything.

A little high-pitched bark makes me look down.

It's Mitzi the chihuahua, sniffing at me through the gate of Chrystal's house. I used to love taking Mitzi through the woods when Chrystal and I were friends, letting her be a proper dog, splashing through muddy puddles and chasing balls.

I hold my hand through the bars. Mitzi sniffs and bats my hand with her soft little head. Something makes me look up and my heart lurches. Lorna is at the window with baby Daniel. His face breaks into a lovely gummy smile; Lorna kisses his black curly head, sees me and waves Daniel's hand at me. I miss him.

I blow Daniel kisses then continue homeward along the yellow brick road. Gradually, the Russian-doll houses get smaller and smaller until I reach mine. Judy and the yellow brick road vanish. It's just me, and I'm sooooo late.

I take a deep breath and, as I step towards

my front door, Sid from Rise and Shine taps me on the shoulder, giving me a fright.

'Come to tea, Bee,' he says with a smile.

'I will, Sid, soon,' I lie.

He whistles a little tune as he disappears into the night. I reach into my bag, then remember I left my key lying on the hall carpet this morning.

Before I have a chance to knock on the door, it opens. Dad stands there scowling.

'Get inside. NOW,' he growls.

12

Dad's muddy brown eyes glare at me. I can smell beer; he's been in the pub. My heart shrinks – his beer talk is nosy, prying. Like a policeman questioning a burglar.

'Get in now,' he says again.

I dodge under Dad's arm, throw my school bag next to the umbrella stand and make for the stairs. Tripping over my feet on the carpet, I scramble up the rickety steps, reaching for my bedroom.

'STOP RIGHT THERE, YOUNG LADY.'

I stop. I turn. He beckons me with his finger. I stumble, jelly-tummied, back down the stairs.

'In there,' he says, pointing to the dining room.

Mum sits at the table, her massive baggy

blue jumper rolled up at the sleeves, running her hands through her spiky red hair. 'Bee,' she says, jumping up and clattering the plates with their remains of sausage and mash and trifle. 'What have you done to your knees?'

'Just tripped up,' I say, pulling my stripy socks over them.

'How many times, Bee? When you are out with Chrystal, you have to let us know. We phoned the house but there was no answer and their car wasn't in their drive, so we knew you must be watching her at gymnastics or something. That's fine. But you have to tell us where you are.'

'Yes,' says Dad, putting his arm around my shoulder, 'it's great that you're friends with the mayor's daughter . . .'

I shake his arm off and don't need to dig deep for my best *you are meant to be my mum and dad, and you don't even know that I am not friends with bendy tap-dancing freak any more, and I am utterly, utterly, heartbroken because Chrystal used to be my best friend in the whole wide world* face. It comes naturally.

Let them believe I was with Chrystal, I think. *I don't care! I'm not going to tell them that I was with Moon-Star in the woods.*

'Well,' I say, 'if you bought me a phone, I could phone to tell you where I am, couldn't I? I can't keep asking to borrow other people's. It's rude using up other people's credit and battery and things.'

'Don't be cheeky to your dad,' says Mum. 'We were worried. Have you eaten?'

'Yes thanks, full up,' I say.

'Sit down,' says Dad.

I slam myself into the chair.

'What did you do at school today?' he asks, like he cares.

'Learning,' I say.

'Learning what?' he says.

'Just things,' I say.

'Bee . . .' warns Mum, spooning some trifle from a big bowl in the middle of the table into a dish for me. 'Dad is just trying to take an interest. Tell us what you've been up to. Here, have a bit of this.'

I open my mouth to tell them about our new boy, Moon-Star, but Dad, as usual, changes the subject before I can even speak. I take a large mouthful of creamy trifle instead. It's scrummy.

'So, Burt and Alfie were saying in the Dog and Duck that the mayor wants to move the old lady in the woods on. A good thing too,' says Dad.

The trifle sticks in my throat.

'But where will she go?' says Mum. 'I don't see why they can't let her live out her days there.' I love my mum for this.

'Nonsense!' says Dad. 'That piece of land has too much potential.'

'Well, it isn't just an old lady in the woods. Her grandson is living with her and he's in my class and he has to stay there,' I blurt out.

'Grandson? What grandson?'

'Moon-Star,' I say. 'Moon-Star Higgins.'

Dad spits trifle everywhere.

'Moon-Star! What kind of ridiculous name is that?'

'It's a wondrous name and it's not nearly

as ridiculous as Beatrix Daffodil Tulip Chrysanthemum Rose Edwards.'

I glare at Dad. He glowers back. It's a stand-off. Neither of us move an inch.

'Please,' says Mum, wringing her hands. 'Don't let's start all this up again. Can't we just all sit round the table eating trifle like a normal family, for once?'

But Dad is still glaring at me. 'Get your books,' he says.

I go into the hall and collect my school bag.

'Please, Mark,' says Mum, 'just let Bee eat her trifle. It's been a long day.'

He starts rifling through my school books, flicking through the pages. 'What work have you done today? Show me.'

'I haven't got anything to show you,' I say. 'We did a literacy test but we had to hand that in obviously and . . . and . . .' I suddenly don't want to tell him I was in the sickbay for hours. 'I was looking after Moon-Star all day,' I lie.

'You!' snorted Dad, smiling. 'You, look after anyone? Oh, Bee, fancy putting you in charge of the new boy. Did you lose this Moon-Star like you lose everything else?'

My eyes prickle.

'And what's this?' he says, screwing up his nose and fishing my horse-chewed sponsor form out of my bag, as if it carried the bubonic plague or one of the other historical diseases that Mrs Partridge is always banging on about.

'It's my form for a sponsored swim. I'm entering it to raise money for the old people at the Rise and Shine Happy Home.'

Dad's face crumples and he starts to laugh. 'How can you do a sponsored swim? You can't swim!' Then he roars until tears are pouring down his face. Mum just looks sad. 'That is the funniest thing I've heard in ages,' he continues. 'You should do a sponsored losing things instead. I'll tell you what, Bee, if you do the sponsored swim I WILL buy you a phone!'

He marches into the kitchen with my form and I follow him and watch as he pins it to the fridge with the honeybee magnet I bought Mum for Mother's Day.

'It will give me a laugh every time I see it. Brilliant! A sponsored swim, eh?'

I follow him back into the dining room.

'Bee,' says Mum, shooting Dad a look. 'Do you think this is quite wise? I am sure there are other things you can do to help the old people.'

I stare from Mum to Dad then from Dad to Mum. My anger crackles.

'Great-Gran Beatrix said I can do anything I set my mind to,' I whisper. 'And I can and I will.'

The crackle gets louder.

'And not that you are interested, but I had an asthma attack today!'

Then the crackle explodes and I can't control it. I can't stop myself.

'Chrystal and the others chased me and I had an asthma attack! Because – not that you have even noticed – I'm not friends with Chrystal any more. In fact, she is my enemy. AND it was *that* old lady in the woods who healed me and gave me tea, and I met a horse called Bob and—'

I bite my lip hard before I blurt out anything about the travellers' pact.

Dad went purple. 'Bee. You are NOT to go in the woods with those people. Do you hear me? You are not to go anywhere near them.'

'Didn't you hear anything I just told you?' I glare at Dad, before storming out of the room and stomping upstairs to my bedroom.

Dad shouts up the stairs after me. 'You will stay away from those people, do you hear?'

I slam my bedroom door and fling myself on top of my *Wizard of Oz* quilt, kicking off my DMs in the process.

I'm angry, but I try to calm myself by looking round at my bedroom and all my wondrous things. I styled my room with Mum and Great-Gran Beatrix's help, and we made one half all about films and the other half all about bees. Dad thinks it looks ridiculous, but he doesn't know what he's talking about! To me, it's a place where I can escape into my own special world, where no one can laugh at me or shatter my dreams.

Great-Gran Beatrix covered the wall next to my bed in honey-coloured felt and stuck loads of felt bees and beehives to it. I straighten one of the giant beehives. The biggest, most beautiful felt bee of all, the queen, is outside the hive, surrounded by the drones and worker bees that serve her. Each felt bee has a different personality to me. Some work as nannies, looking after the baby bees, some guard the hive, some collect nectar. They are working, working, working.

Great-Gran Beatrix and I also made big brightly coloured felt flowers for the bees to enjoy – daffodils, tulips, chrysanthemums and roses, all the flowers in my name. I stroke the queen bee's wings. My one yellow curtain and my one black curtain flutter in the evening breeze. I'm already feeling calmer.

I wander over to my chair, which has my red feather boa draped across it. 'Director' is written across the back of the chair, like the ones they have on film sets. My dressing table is like a film star's too, with light bulbs around the mirror and pots of glittery make-up and proper grown-up brushes. It makes me feel like a real actress. I arrange the pots of make-up and brushes and lipsticks into a rainbow of colours. It makes me think of Chrystal. One of our best things to do was play make-up. I miss those times.

Shaking the sad thoughts out of my ears, I step back to admire my film-star wall. Mum and I painted it black with white stripes, like a film clapperboard. My own clapperboard hangs in the middle of the wall, and all my favourite black and white photos of Judy and Marilyn surround it.

Flinging my red feather boa round my shoulders, I smile like Marilyn. If I had a phone I would take selfies.

There is a knock on the door. 'Bee,' says Mum, through the wood. 'Bee, love. Can I come in?'

I don't answer.

'Come on, Bee, don't upset yourself. Your dad is only showing he cares . . . He just wants what's best for you.'

Silence. I don't move a muscle.

'Bee, would you like me to come in and brush your hair?'

I hold my breath. More silence.

'All right then, Bee. Good night; I love you.'

I wait until I hear her go back downstairs.

Then I remember the muslin bag Old Alice gave me to help me sleep and fish it out of my pocket. It smells of lavender and autumn mist.

I place the little bag under my pillow and grab a pen and my bee notebook with its silky padded cover. I drop the boa in a little feathery pile at the end of my bed and climb under my quilt, then I find an empty page and copy down what I learned from Old Alice:

Manuka honey is good for healing.
Honey is good for my asthma.

Great-Gran Beatrix filled the notebook with wise sayings about bees in her lovely handwriting. I close my eyes, flick through the pages and then stop. I peep through my lashes.

It has landed on her favourite one.

The busy bee has no time for sorrow. **William Blake**

It gives me a jolt. I have no time for feeling sorry for myself. I have to learn how to swim.

I start to write.

Dear Great-Gran Beatrix,

Today I met a boy. His name is Moon-Star Higgins. I wish so much that I could bring him to say hello to you. I don't think I am very good at talking to boys but Moon-Star is different. And I think that you would like him very much. In fact, I think you most probably have made your mind up about him already because I know that you are watching over me from your star.

My heart is broken that I did not learn to swim before you died. I'm sorry for letting you down so badly, but I know that Moon-Star is going to help me keep my promise to you. I know that you would still want me to learn to swim.

Love from your unique, one and only great-granddaughter,

Bee xxxxx

I pad across the dark room and lean out of my window. Up in the sky is the largest, twinkliest star. Great-Gran Beatrix is definitely smiling at me. I hold the book open and imagine the words swimming up to the crescent moon and spreading across the sky for Great-Gran Beatrix to read. I blow her star a kiss.

13

Thought storms wrestle in my brain when I wake up the next morning. Lightning strikes and I remember the pact by the Promise Tree that can never be broken.

But what if Moon-Star skips school? He'll be taken away and the pact will be broken and . . . and . . . and I can't bear to think about it. I stretch my legs and flinch – the cuts on my knees from yesterday still sting.

I wish I could stay safe in my bedroom for ever and not have to worry about sponsored swims, and whether Moon-Star will turn up for school or not, and going to tea with the old people, and, well, everything.

I squint sleepily across the room at my

hatstand. My heart jolts as I see the one empty peg. Great-Gran Beatrix knew she wouldn't be here for my next birthday so she asked Mum to order me a special hat for the last peg – a swimming hat decorated with rubber bees and wings that flap from each side. But I can't bear to look at it – it's a reminder that I've failed, failed, failed! So it's stuffed in a drawer, where I can't see it. Only, I still know it's there. Sometimes I dream of that swimming hat, calling to me from its hiding place.

The notes of a blackbird's early morning song tell me it's time to get up. I fling back my faded *Wizard of Oz* quilt cover. Mum said that she would buy me a new cover, one more suitable for a growing young lady, but I don't want a new one. It's babyish, but I'm never getting rid of it, not ever.

I stretch out my sore knees and pad across the room, opening my bedroom door to listen out for the sound of Mum and Dad downstairs. The yellow glittery star on my door twinkles at me. Famous actresses had stars on their dressing-room doors, so Great-Gran Beatrix said I should have one too, because I am her star.

There is silence. Mum and Dad can't be up yet. All that arguing must have tired them out.

The blackbird starts singing again. I need to hurry and get dressed then I can knock for Moon-Star, walk him to school and make sure he keeps his side of the pact. But Dad's words, '*You will stay away from those people*,' shiver in my tummy. I have to get out of the house before Dad sees me and starts going on again.

I drag on my uniform and choose today's hat – a brown velvet top hat that smells of Christmas log fires and glints red when it catches the light. When I tried it on for the first time, on my eighth birthday, it was so big it fell over my eyes and Great-Gran Beatrix and I laughed till our bellies hurt. She sent it away to London to have padding fitted and now it fits so perfectly, it's like wearing a pair of slippers on my head. It's so high it makes me walk tall. It makes me walk proud.

I place the top hat on my head so it's as

straight as straight can be and creep down the rickety stairs.

No time for breakfast. Through the open kitchen door, the sponsor form mocks me from its place on the fridge, but I ignore it, grab my school bag and my key from the hall table and tiptoe out of the front door. I shut my eyes so I don't have to see the Rise and Shine Happy Home for Older People.

A banging on the window behind me makes me jump. I look up and see Dad. 'Wait there,' he mouths.

Dad springs out of the front door. 'I'm taking you.'

My heart drops to my toes. How am I going to get Moon-Star to school now?

Dad strides to our battered blue car and opens the back door. 'Get in,' he says.

Despite my heavy heart, I dig really, really deep and give him my very best *I will be really seriously ill and might get the bubonic plague if I don't walk to school and get some fresh air* face.

'Stop pulling silly faces and get in the car,' says Dad.

'It's very kind of you, Dad,' I say politely, 'but it's very important I get my daily exercise and walk through the woods to school.'

'Get in,' he says. 'Do you think I was born yesterday? You're going to see that Moon boy.'

I scramble into the car.

'Put your seat belt on, ducky.'

I jump. Mabel from Rise and Shine is poking her head through the open car window. I swear those old people are stalking me.

'Come to tea,' she says.

'I will,' I lie.

We drive up the road, past the Russian-doll houses. Dad jolts to a stop to allow Chrystal's mum to pull out of her driveway in her Porsche. He waves to her.

Chrystal and I lock eyes for a dot of a second. I turn my head to the big tree in her front garden. We used to sit up in its branches dreaming of what magical stories the future would bring us.

Dad drives over the bridge and I panic that the waters will get me if I don't do my twenty-five hops. Even though I am in a car, I *have* to do them, I just have to. So I close my eyes and tap one foot on the car floor and count really, really quickly. As I say 'twenty-five' I open my eyes, just as we reach the other side. I've done it! My heart sings.

We drive on through the trees and towards the clearing. My eyes search frantically for Moon-Star. There's a bed sheet drying on the branch of a tree. Bob trots into view and shies away from its fluttering whiteness.

'Moon-Star, where are you?' I say under my breath.

The car skids to a halt and swerves. I jolt forward, the seat belt cutting into me. Dad leaps out of the car, runs in front of it and scoops up a little bundle of hissing grey fluff. It's the kitten.

Dad gently strokes it, talking to it all the time. Why can't he be gentle like that with me? From behind a tree steps Old Alice. I hold my breath. Please, please, please, please, Dad, don't be rude. Dad nods a greeting at her. Old Alice nods one back and holds out her arms for the kitten. She turns to me and gives me the titchiest of winks, so small it could ride on the crest of a breeze, but I saw it.

Dad didn't. Ha!

Then she disappears into the trees.

What does it mean? Is Moon-Star coming to school? Is he not? I search the memory of her face for hidden clues but find none.

'That was a close shave, Bee,' says Dad. 'That kitten's lucky.' And he starts singing that old Kylie song 'I Should Be So Lucky'. He's so embarrassing!

As we pull up outside school, Dad passes me a pound.

'Just in case you need it,' he says. 'Get yourself some sweets.'

'Thanks,' I say, and give him an almost-smile.

'And, Bee, remember you are there to do your own lessons, not look after that Moon boy.'

The almost-smile vanishes. I mutter, 'Bye,' practically fall out of the car and, swinging my bag over my shoulder, walk on to the playing field. I scan the field for Moon-Star, but I can't see him anywhere. I do see Chrystal Kelly, sitting at the far end, by the hedge, a gaggle of girls round her.

There are various games of football being played. Timothy Lee is standing reading a book; they are using him as one of the goalposts. He looks up and blinks at me. I try to dodge the flying footballs, but one hits me smack on my sore knee. I wince and close my ears against the yelling, pushing, shoving boys and girls.

I walk on past, eyes looking in desperation for Moon-Star. He's definitely not here. With a sinking heart, I sit on the grass under a cedar tree on my own.

'Please come to school, Moon-Star, please, please come,' I pray.

He doesn't though. The seconds tick towards the assembly bell.

I watch as Chrystal makes the gaggle of girls around her stand in a circle, ready for a dance-off. Which is her best thing and my worst.

She gets a rhythm going. *Clap-clap stamp. Clap-clap stamp.* One by one, they all take turns

to go in the middle and show off their moves –
then it's Chrystal's turn and she does some
backflips and cartwheels and lands in the splits.
Everyone whoops.

Clap-clap stamp. Clap-clap stamp.

Then Alba and Lily run over to me, grab my
hands and pull me into the middle of the circle.

Clap-clap stamp. Clap-clap stamp.

Clap-clap stamp. Clap-clap stamp.

'Go on then,' mocks Chrystal. 'Show us what
you can do.'

Clap-clap stamp. Clap-clap stamp.

And I feel so awkward and stupid and my
feet feel massive in my clumpy DMs and my
face burns red and I just want to disappear
inside my top hat, like a magician's rabbit. I'd
rather be anywhere else in the world than in
the middle of that circle.

I step to the side and *clap-step* to the other
side and *clap*.

'Are you trying to dance?' smirks Chrystal.

Everyone laughs. I push through the circle
and run back to the cedar tree. Ignoring the

laughter, I get out my bee notebook and flick through the pages. It lands on:

> *The only reason for making a buzzing noise that I know of is because you're a bee … The only reason for being a bee that I know of is making honey … And the only reason for making honey is so I can eat it.*
> **A. A. Milne's The House at Pooh Corner**

My tummy gurgles. I smile. It's Great-Gran Beatrix's way of telling me off for not eating breakfast.

I look up to see that the dance-off has stopped. Chrystal is crunching on an apple.

'Bryony, she's my trainer, says it's essential I get the right nutrients and I don't eat anything that could stop me being a winner,' her voice screeches across the field.

The girls sit round her, drinking in her words with admiration. Suckers! I saw Chrystal in Robson's Newsagent's last week getting a Twix and a packet of Quavers.

'Please, Moon-Star, please,' I say over and over again inside my head. 'Please come to school.'

Mr Gregory walks on to the playing field with a worried-looking woman, who is smartly dressed in black trousers and a red shirt. Mrs Partridge follows them, carrying two mugs of tea on a tray. Mr Gregory's scanning the field for someone and a cold feeling trickles down my spine.

A shadow falls over me. I look up. Chrystal.

'Waiting for your scruffy, dirty boyfriend, are you?' she sneers.

'Who are you calling dirty? And yes he is a boy and he is my *friend* – which is more than you are.'

Mr Gregory, Mrs Partridge and the lady in red walk in our direction, but before they reach us, there's a pounding of hooves and the snapping of twigs and Bob and Moon-Star jump over the fence! Happiness and fear roll together into a tight ball inside me.

Bob snatches the apple from Chrystal's hand and chomps it. She screams. Bob snorts and starts prancing round in circles. I guess Ashton

Junior School Sports Girl of the Year doesn't stretch to equestrian skills. She's always been scared of horses.

'Chrystal, shut up! You're scaring Bob,' I shout, my hands over my ears as she continues to scream.

Mrs Partridge and the lady in red break into a run towards us, tea slopping everywhere.

Moon-Star calms Bob, whispering gentle secrets to him, then he slowly stands up and balances on Bob's back, his arms outstretched.

My grin feels as if it will tear my mouth open as I look up at Moon-Star.

'Stop screaming this instant, Chrystal, you'll frighten this fine animal!' Mr Gregory snaps.

Partridge is fuming. The lady in red looks disapproving.

'He . . . he . . . he took my apple,' sobs Chrystal.

'For goodness' sake, Chrystal, it's what horses eat! You were waving it in the air. Of course he took it,' says Mr Gregory.

In all my school days I've never heard Mr

Gregory talk to Chrystal like this, not ever!

He's boiling angry. Everyone's eyes are on him, waiting to see what's going to happen next.

Mrs Partridge bristles. 'Well, this is disgraceful—'

Mr Gregory holds out a hand to stop her. 'Moon-Star,' says Mr Gregory, 'this lady has come to check up on you.'

'I know who she is,' scowls Moon-Star. 'I'm here, aren't I? What more do you want?'

'Well,' says the lady in the red shirt, 'it's hardly an appropriate way to get to school.'

Then Mr Gregory bursts into a chuckle which becomes a laugh that turns into a bellow.

'This is the most original way of getting to school I have ever seen,' he chokes. 'Whatever it takes to get you into lessons, Moon-Star, whatever it takes.'

Then Mr Gregory turns to Mrs Partridge and the lady in red and says, 'Thank you, both. I will take it from here.'

Mrs Partridge opens and closes her mouth like a goldfish.

'I'll be in touch,' says the lady in red, 'about Moon-Star's progress.'

'Of course,' says Mr Gregory. 'Mrs Partridge, if you would kindly see our visitor to the gate.'

Mr Gregory waits until they walk away from us.

'Now, my lawn could do with a bit of a trim, so how about if we tether . . .'

'Bob,' says Moon-Star, sliding off Bob's back.

'Bob,' says Mr Gregory, stroking the horse on his nose. 'If we tether Bob in my garden, then we can get you into the classroom.'

All the colour vanishes from Moon-Star's face in an instant.

'The pact can never be broken,' I whisper into Moon-Star's ear.

'I know,' he says and we walk over the playing field on either side of Bob, the whole school watching us.

14

Mr Gregory's cottage is surrounded by lovely long grass. As we walk round to it, Mrs Gregory comes out. She's cuddly and plump and is wearing a blue flowery dress.

'Oh my, oh my – he's a beauty,' she says.

Moon-Star beams at her. 'His name's Bob,' he says.

'Well, I'll get Bob some water.' She disappears into a shed, returns with a bucket and fills it from an outside tap.

'Can I leave the bridle with ya?' says Moon-Star, lifting the reins over Bob's head and undoing a buckle at the side, letting the slobbery metal bit drop into his hand.

Mrs Gregory smiles and nods to a hook at

the side of the shed.

Bob wanders over to the bucket. The water slops over the sides as he drinks.

As Moon-Star walks away, I take my chance to talk to Mr Gregory. I tap him on the arm. 'Thank you for letting me come, Mr Gregory. Moon-Star needs to be at school, but he is going to find it so hard.'

Mr Gregory smiles. 'Moon-Star needs a friend. And I think you will be very good at that, Bee.'

'Really?' I whisper.

He nods.

As Moon-Star comes back, he pats his pocket, frowns and pulls out a cloth with something squashed in it.

'Bee, Gran give me this for you – 'tis bread and honey. Said she knows in her bones you won't have eaten breakfast.'

I realise how starving I am and grab it from him.

'I need to get to assembly now,' Mr Gregory says. 'I'll leave you two to settle Bob, but I'll expect you not to be late for your first class. Oh and, Bee, that is a fine top hat, but you know the school rules. Please make sure you take it off before you go into lessons.'

I grin at him, snatching it off my head and shaking out my hair.

'Yes, sir,' I say.

As Mr Gregory walks back to school, I sit on the grass and stuff the mashed-up bread and honey down me '*like there's no tomorrow*', as Great-Gran Beatrix used to say.

Mrs Gregory watches us through the cottage window as she washes up.

We run with Bob as he trots through the grass, nudging us with his nose. I take a quick puff of my inhaler to keep the elephant at bay.

Bob rolls in the grass and we lie, resting our heads on him, watching a honeybee collect nectar from the pink blossom on a tree.

I remember the bee landing on Moon-Star's finger the first time I met him.

'Moon-Star,' I ask, 'can all your family charm the bees? I've seen Old Alice . . .'

'Yep,' says Moon-Star, 'we are nature and nature is us.'

'I love bees – wish I could do it.'

'You can collect honey with me if you want,' says Moon-Star, grinning.

A sharp tap at the window makes us look up. Mrs Gregory points to her watch.

'Assembly's over, got to go to class,' I say, brushing the bits of grass off me.

Moon-Star drags his feet the whole way, so by the time we get to our classroom, Mrs Partridge has already started the history lesson. It's about witches in olden times.

'Oh come in, Moon-Star, Bee. Um yes, if you sit . . .'

'He can sit next to me, miss,' I say, walking to my desk. There is an empty space next to it. No one will sit next to me now that Chrystal has made me her enemy.

Moon-Star sits down and the class snigger. I give them my best *you are all so immature* face. I draw another bee tattoo on my arm and half listen as Mrs Partridge drones on.

Out of the corner of my eye I see Moon-Star's

hands and feet jiggling. I grab a bit of paper and resting it on my knee under the desk I write: W is for WITCH and I draw my best picture of a witch flying against the moon with my fluorescent pens.

I nudge Moon-Star and put the picture on his lap. I give him a pencil.

He mouths, 'Witch,' and writes W I T C H underneath.

Then I draw a moon and star and colour them in with my yellow fluorescent pen.

I write MOON-STAR.

Then I draw another witch and an arrow and write MRS PARTRIDGE

I nudge Moon-Star and point from my drawing to our teacher. He sniggers.

Partridge swivels round. I swear she has actual eyes in the back of her head.

'WILL YOU LISTEN, MOON-STAR AND BEATRIX DAFFODIL TU—'

'Please, Mrs Partridge, I have been listening.'

'OK then, Beatrix, stand up and tell the class what you know about witches in history.'

My mind goes blank, then inspiration shimmers and I grab it hard with both hands.

'In Salem in America,' I begin, 'three girls, Ann, Betty and Abigail, started going hysterical and acting weird and saying they saw witches. They blamed Tituba, a lady who looked after them, and everyone accused of being a witch blamed someone else, and so on and so on, but they were making it up and because of them nineteen women were accused of witchcraft and hanged.'

I plonk myself back down in my chair.

Mrs Partridge opens and shuts her mouth a few times before stammering, 'Beatrix . . . how . . . how did you know all that?'

'Because, Mrs Partridge,' I say, putting on my best *I am just so intelligent* face, 'because,' I say again, enjoying the moment, 'Arthur Miller the playwright wrote a play about it called *The Crucible* and he was married to Marilyn Monroe.'

She glares at me. 'I might have known,' says Mrs Partridge, rolling her eyes. 'I might have known it would have something to do with silly film stars; now get your head out of the clouds and listen, please.'

'Mrs Partridge,' says Moon-Star, 'does it matter how Bee knows the answer to your old history question, as long as she knows?'

I gasp and bite my lip, my heart fluttering. Moon-Star gives me a wink.

Mrs Partridge goes red. 'Er . . . well . . . I suppose not. Now, where was I . . .?'

My words dart round in my brain. Nineteen women hanged just cos Abigail, Betty and Ann made it all up.

As Mrs Partridge talks, I think about how many ladies throughout history might have been accused of being witches and were burned or drowned. Sometimes it was just because they had a gift to predict the weather, or were blamed if a crop failed, or sometimes just cos they were seen muttering to themselves.

Old Alice, with her charming of the bees, and living in her wagon surrounded by all her cats, would definitely have been accused of witchcraft in olden times. They crossed women's arms and tied their thumbs to their toes and threw them in a river. If the waters got them and dragged them down they were innocent but if they floated they were witches and they would be dragged out of the water and burned at the stake or executed. Either way, they died a horrible death. Chrystal and I called Old Alice a witch. I am a completely terrible person.

I feel bad about windbag Partridge too – she may be annoying all of the time, but I don't hate her enough for the waters to get her, so I grab my fluorescent pen and start to scrub out her name by my drawing of the witch. It's not nice calling people witches, even when it's Partridge.

'Class,' says Mrs Partridge, 'I want you to write a story about a witch. You have ten minutes to chat to your neighbour about your ideas first.'

There is talk and chatter as people grab exercise books and pens. Moon-Star's fingers claw at the wooden desk. He starts to make his chair judder, then scrapes it back and begins pacing round the classroom really quickly.

I jump up and gently lead him back to his chair.

Mrs Partridge watches.

'Can't write no story,' hisses Moon-Star.

'We're going to do it together,' I whisper in his ear.

Moon-Star hoists himself on to his desk, his foot kicking the wooden leg. I can feel prickly fear radiating from him.

Mrs Partridge frowns at us. Oh no, he's going to be in trouble . . .

'Where does our witch live?' I say quickly, trying to distract him.

He kicks the desk harder and faster.

'MOON-STAR HIGGINS! SIT AT YOUR DESK PROPERLY!' shouts Mrs Partridge.

Moon-Star sits on the edge of his chair, wild panic in his eyes like he's a trapped beast.

'She don't live nowhere,' he says, 'she wanders round from village to village and sleeps in barns and people think she brings 'em luck with the weather.'

'That's brilliant,' I say. 'Maybe one farmer won't let her sleep in his barn.'

'Yer, he don't like travelling folks,' says Moon-Star, rocking on his chair. Then he slides to the floor and actually sits under the desk.

There's nothing else for it. I slide on to the floor in front of him. I hear the class snigger.

'Quiet, class,' says Mrs Partridge. 'Get on with your work.'

From my position on the floor, I can see Partridge's red pointy shoes and wrinkly tights making their way towards us. I hold my breath.

Then Chrystal's voice rings out, 'On the dirty floor with your dirty boyfriend!'

'That's enough, Chrystal Saffron Kelly!' says Mrs Partridge, and the red pointy shoes and wrinkly tights go marching off.

My cheeks are on fire with embarrassment. Moon-Star rolls out from under the desk and strides towards the door.

Panicked, I chase after him. 'Remember the pact,' I whisper.

He closes his eyes, shivers, then walks back to his desk and squashes himself behind it. The class silently watches.

I start to write down Moon-Star's ideas and, before long, everyone loses interest in us and a gentle whispering of witch stories fills the air.

Then I hear something else brewing – a murmur of 'Move on. Move on.'

It's coming from Chrystal's direction and now everyone's joining in.

It's getting louder and louder.

Moon-Star looks around him, trapped like a fox caught in headlights.

Then there's a neigh and Bob sticks his head through the window next to Chrystal's desk. Chrystal shrieks as Bob grabs her exercise book in his mouth and starts chewing. She runs to the other side of the class, squealing.

The class's whispers turn to hysterical laughter and we all laugh and laugh and laugh, ignoring Mrs Partridge's yells to 'QUIETEN DOWN.'

But Chrystal's voice cuts through the laughter. 'Let's see what my father has to say about this, disrupting our education. Old Alice and her dirty, scruffy grandson should just be *moved on.*'

Moon-Star jumps up, kicks the fallen chair out of the way, leaps on to Chrystal's desk and pushes Bob's nose out of the window. Then he scrabbles out after his horse and disappears.

There is a forever silence.

I realise I'm standing, though I can't feel my legs, and everyone is staring at me. I hear screamed words and they seem to be coming from far, far away, only then I realise they're coming from my mouth.

'LOOK WHAT YOU'VE DONE!' my voice spirals to the top of a mountain. 'He's gone, and it's all your fault, Chrystal! I hate you. I hate all of you. You make me sick!'

'Get out of my classroom, Bee. Now,' says Mrs Partridge with deathly calm.

So I do.

15

I grab my bag and stampede down the corridor,
a plan already forming in my brain. I don't care
if my elbows and knees are joggling everywhere.
I've got to get to Mr Gregory's office before
Partridge does.

I burst through the door. Mr Gregory's on
his computer.

'Please, sir, you have to come. It's Moon-Star!'
A wheeze escapes. I grapple for my inhaler and
take a puff.

'Bee, take it easy. What's happened? Tell me.'

I tell him everything. 'I think we'll find him
in your garden, sir, with Bob,' I finish.

As we walk towards the cottage I tell Mr
Gregory my plan.

When we enter the garden, Moon-Star has his back to us, putting on Bob's bridle.

He buries his face in Bob's coat. 'I couldn't do school,' he says. 'I tried, cos I promised you, Bee, but I just can't do it.'

Before I can speak, Mr Gregory jumps in. 'How about we strike a deal, Moon-Star,' he says. 'You and Bee can do some reading and writing practice outside today. Tomorrow, you come back into the classroom and try again.'

Moon-Star turns round and shrugs his shoulders.

'Now, will you both come with me, please,' the head teacher says.

It is morning break when we get back. As we go into the classroom, I can hear chatter and cheer from the playground and the smack of balls kicked against walls.

Mrs Partridge is on her laptop. 'Oh, I was just emailing you, Mr Gregory. I simply can't have this behaviour in my classroom.'

'Mrs Partridge, I have addressed this

morning's unfortunate incident and I know you will be delighted to hear that Bee has come up with a solution,' says Mr Gregory. 'Now, Bee, what do you have in mind?'

'Well,' I say, 'if Moon-Star sits by the window, with me next to him, then I think . . .' I turn to Moon-Star, 'I think maybe you won't feel so trapped.'

Moon-Star nods at me and slowly sits down.

'Can we keep the window open?' he says. 'Just in case I gotta go.'

'Yes of course,' says Mr Gregory, 'whatever makes you feel comfortable.'

I sit next to Moon-Star. He smiles at me.

'But, Mr Gregory,' simpers Mrs Partridge, 'that's Chrystal's place.'

'I think you'll agree, Mrs Partridge,' Mr Gregory says, 'that it is a good idea to keep Moon-Star and Bee together. This friendship is important to both of them. I see Bee on her own more than I would like.'

'Of course,' says Mrs Partridge. 'Whatever you think is best, Mr Gregory.'

'And I don't see any reason why you can't bring that fine horse to school, Moon-Star, providing you dismount and walk with him through the school gates and then take him straight to my garden. Would that help you settle in?'

Moon-Star grins.

The door bangs open and Chrystal runs in. She stops when she sees the head teacher. 'Oh sorry, Mr Gregory, I want to get my— What are they doing sitting in my place?'

'I'm afraid it's not your place any more, Chrystal. Moon-Star will be sitting there from now on.'

'But—'

'But nothing, Chrystal. It's all been arranged.'

She tosses her hair and turns her head to us so that Mr Gregory can't see, and mouths, 'You wait.'

Moon-Star puts his hand on my shoulder and glares at her, mouthing back, 'Just you try.'

Back in the rose garden, we sit and watch as petals fall like red raindrops, the beautiful scent tickling my nose.

I dip my hand into my school bag. It closes over the silky cover of my bee book. I dilly-dally between shall I shan't I share my secrets with Moon-Star? I go for 'shall' and lift the book out of my bag. *We're meant to be doing reading and writing after all*, I think to myself.

'Moon-Star,' I say shyly. 'I've got a special book to show you.'

I hold it out to him. I know it's OK to show Moon-Star cos I know he won't be able to read my private writing anyway but then I feel mean for thinking such thoughts.

'It's my bee notebook. My Great-Gran Beatrix left it to me before she died. It's full of her wisdom.'

Moon-Star takes the book in his hands and carefully turns it over, then he opens it and looks down at one of the sayings.

'This is extraordinary,' he says.

'It's wondrous,' I say.

'She must have loved you more than life itself to make you such a book,' says Moon-Star.

I nod, my eyes prickling. I quickly look down at the grass. A tear escapes and trickles down my chin.

Moon-Star wipes it away from my cheek with his thumb.

'Tell me what it says,' he whispers.

I read:

> *The men of experiment are like the ant; they only collect and use. But the bee gathers its materials from the flowers of the garden and of the field, but transforms and digests it by a power of its own.* **Leonardo da Vinci**

'That's us, see,' Moon-Star points out. 'We are like bees – we gotta use our inner power to transform. You with your swimming and me with my letters.'

We sit there in the long grass for ages, while I read Moon-Star the secrets of the bees. And our hands nearly touch but not quite.

16

I arrive home buzzing after my day with Moon-Star and I'm just turning my bag upside down for my key when I hear, 'Hi, Bee, how are you doing?'

Lorna, the Kellys' nanny, is wheeling baby Daniel down the road.

I run over to them.

'Go on,' she says, 'have a cuddle. I think Daniel misses you.'

He blows me a raspberry smile. I clasp his warm little body in my arms; he smells of apples and summer days.

Lorna's very pretty, her long black hair pulled back into a ponytail. I smile at her. She used to let me bath Daniel when Chrystal and I were friends. Daniel grabs my hair and I laugh and wince as I pull it from his grip, leaving a handful of red hairs in his tight little fist.

'Bye-bye, Daniel.' I wave as Lorna wheels him away, feeling a raindrop of sadness in my heart.

As I let myself into the house with my front door key, I hear Mum singing in the kitchen.

'Is that you, darling? Lasagne and chips for tea.'

'Yum, it smells gorgeous,' I say.

'Dad is working late, so we're going to eat without him,' she calls.

Yes! This day just got better.

Happy thoughts of Moon-Star and Bob and red gypsy wagons and the little grey kitten tumble about in my head, then stop with a tummy kick when I see THE SPONSOR FORM pinned to the fridge.

I'd been so proud of myself for helping Moon-Star with his letters that I'd almost forgotten my side of the pact that can never ever be broken.

How am I going to learn to swim? I sit down at the dinner table with jelly legs. Even though lasagne and chips is my top favourite dinner I can't eat that much of it. I really can't.

Mum is still singing and looks brighter, sharper and less faded than she is when Dad is arguing with her. She is so relaxed when Dad's not here. He always moans on about the mess when she paints, but Mum *loves* painting. A half-finished landscape of a beach and a rough sea rests on an easel in the corner of the dining room, little pots of paint scattered around everywhere. The sea looks so real it makes me shiver.

Mum smiles at me. 'What secrets are you hiding in that head of yours, Bee?'

'Secrets can never be told, Mum, or they wouldn't be secrets,' I whisper in her ear, then run up the stairs to my bedroom.

Judy and Marilyn smile down at me. I bet they could swim. I scramble out of my boring grey school uniform and pull on my bumblebee onesie, fling my red feather boa over my shoulders and reach for my pink 1920s woollen hat with the blue knitted flower on the side. It smells of cinnamon.

I love this hat; it's so cosy but it makes me look and feel like an actress from one of those old silent films. I pose in front of the mirror for a bit, then I swap the woollen hat for my dark brown felt trilby with the red feather tucked into its band. Judy Garland wore a trilby when she sang 'Get Happy' in the film *Summer Stock*. Great-Gran Beatrix used to sing 'Get Happy' to me when I didn't want to go to school and had a mood on. She'd sing it and sing it till I'd feel a giggle rising, and before I knew it I was singing along with her and humming it all the way to school. She bought me this hat for my ninth birthday.

I tip the trilby over one eye and admire the effect in my dressing-table mirror. An explosion of confidence blazes through me. I feel just like Judy Garland. I am a star.

One by one, I try on all of my special hats, finishing with my solid black bowler that grips my head with a hug. It feels downy to stroke and has the most perfect white silk daisy on the brim. It's one of a kind, as Great-Gran Beatrix had it specially made for my tenth birthday.

She told me to stand in front of my dressing-table mirror and shut my eyes, then she placed it on my head and tilted it back. '*Open your eyes, Bee*,' she whispered in my ear. '*See what dazzling style you have.*'

I tilt the bowler hat back now, as Great-Gran Beatrix did, then I dig into my virtual scrapbook and pull my best acting faces in the mirror.

A snort makes me jump and turn. Moon-Star is peeping through the window.

I scream.

'Bee! Are you OK?' Mum shouts up the stairs.

As Moon-Star pulls himself up on to the window sill, his foot slips, so I have to grab him and haul him in.

'I'm fine, Mum,' I shout down to her. 'I dropped a pot of make-up. Just being clumsy as usual.'

'As long as you're OK,' she calls back to me.

I wait till I hear her walk back into the kitchen.

'How . . .' I say, 'how did you get up here?'

'What do you mean "how"? I shimmied up

the drainpipe,' Moon-star tells me, as if it's the most obvious thing in the world.

Suddenly I feel awkward with him standing here, in my bedroom.

I hold my breath as he looks round, hands in his jean pockets, his pale-blue shirt half tucked in, half tucked out of his jeans, taking in my private world – Marilyn and Judy, my bees, my mirror, my hatstand. He whistles under his breath, then he plonks himself on my bed and laughs at my *Wizard of Oz* quilt.

'Laugh if you want – I've had it since I was about five. Great-Gran Beatrix gave it to me and I'm not throwing it away, not ever.'

'Who are you, Dorothy?'

'Of course,' I say, 'and you, Moon-Star, are the Scarecrow.'

'Why? Cos my school uniform's a hand-me-down?' He laughs, but I see a wave of hurt flicker across his face.

'No, no, no.' I feel sick to have hurt his feelings. 'It's because he doesn't think he's got a brain, but he has – he is so smart.'

Moon-Star thinks a moment then grins. 'That's OK then. And now, Dorothy, it's time for your swimming lesson.'

'What? Now?' The ground goes from beneath me, but I know I have to keep my side of the pact.

'Come on, Bee, get a wiggle on, we've got a lot to do.'

'OK, but you have to shut your eyes,' I say.

I wait till his eyes are firmly shut tight cos my dreaded swimming costume is in my underwear drawer and I don't want Moon-Star to see my knickers.

I grab my inhaler from my school bag and run across the landing to the airing cupboard, grabbing some towels to wrap up my costume and inhaler.

Back in the bedroom, Moon-Star's eyes are still shut. 'Can I open them?' he says.

'Wait,' I say and grab my trilby with the feather and put it on Moon-Star's head. I stuff my feet into my DMs.

'Look,' I whisper. He opens his eyes and

we look at our reflections. As I stand next to Moon-Star in my bowler hat, bumblebee onesie and red feather boa, I think that there is no one else on the planet who would wear such things.

'We have dazzling style,' I whisper, for Moon-Star looks so fine with his trilby and feather.

'Come on,' he says, 'time to swim. I'll help you down.'

'What?' I say. 'Out of the window?'

He grins. 'I'll show you. Bob is waiting for us . . .'

He stuffs some pillows under my quilt to make it look like the shape of a body.

'Your ma and da'll think you're asleep if they look in.'

Then he tucks my towel bundle under his arm, heaves himself through the window and shimmies down the drainpipe to the roof that sticks out over the kitchen. I stay on the window sill.

'Come on,' he hisses, putting the towel bundle down and reaching up to me.

I turn and grab the drainpipe. I feel his arms grab my waist as he guides me down, one foot over the other. The feather boa is tickling my nose. Then I scramble over the roof behind Moon-Star, until he disappears from view. I sit down, shuffling my bottom towards where he vanished and peep over the edge. He is standing on a pile of boxes with my towel tucked under his arm again. As I heave myself down, the bowler hat tips over my eyes, but soon I've made it to the ground in one piece.

We creep across the grass, climb over the fence and race to Bob, who is busy eating Dad's hedge. Moon-Star gives me a leg up on to Bob's back and climbs behind me, wedging my towel bundle between us so I can hold on to Bob with both hands.

I rearrange the feather boa, shake out my long red hair, tilt back my bowler and grin as we ride across the field.

'Relax your legs as you wrap 'em around Bob. When you do riding without a saddle, you should feel your seat bones on either side of

Bob's spine.'

I nod, feeling the horse's power beneath me.

'If you ride Bob, it will make your legs stronger for swimming, Bee – you'll see.'

'Where are we going?' I whisper.

'To the lake.'

My heart catapults up into the back of my throat.

'No – not the lake. The waters'll get me.'

'Bob and I are going to look after you, Bee.'

When we reach the bridge, I start to count to twenty-five, even though I'm on horseback. I can't help it.

'What are you doing?' whispers Moon-Star in my ear.

'Nothing,' I lie. He'll think I'm crazy if I tell him.

We go by Old Alice's red wagon and head down the path, past the hives. It's starting to get dark. As we ride beneath the Promise Tree, I reach up to the oak's branches. The leaves tickle my fingers.

Now I can hear the running water of the

river. I've never explored this part of the woods before. The trees are so close together but Bob seems sure of his footing. Moon-Star loosens the reins and Bob guides us through – then stops. I gasp. There, in the moonlight, is a secret pool. The river flows into it and then flows out the other side. The half moon and the stars reflect in the ripples – it's wondrous.

'Stick your foot out flat,' says Moon-Star. He steps lightly on the top of my foot, using it like a stirrup to dismount from Bob. He turns around and lifts me down.

I'm shaking so much as I get changed behind a willow tree. I shut my eyes, count to three, open them and step out through the drooping willow leaves. I take a deep breath and walk over to Bob, the wet grass tickling my feet. Moon-Star has stripped down to his shorts. I look at my toes.

'Don't be shy, Bee,' he says. 'Now, hop back up on Bob – he's coming swimming with us.'

He gives me a leg up, on to Bob's back.

But even the lovely warm feeling of Bob's

coat under my legs doesn't stop me from shaking.

'Bee,' says Moon-Star, walking beside the horse. 'Bob and me's got you safe. Do you trust us?'

I nod. I'm terrified I might cry if I speak.

'But you gotta keep calm; Bob don't like people panicking on his back, it makes him jumpy.'

'I'll try,' I say, 'but I don't want the waters to get me.'

'They won't, Bee.'

I try to believe his words but I'm still quivering.

'This edge bit here is shallow, so we are going for a little paddle, like we are at the beach.'

'OK,' I squeak and hold my breath.

I hold the reins like Moon-Star shows me. He walks by my side, leading Bob down to the edge of the pool. Bob steps in and snorts. Up and down we walk, the water lapping beneath me but, to my relief, not quite touching my toes.

'Right, we are going for a trot. Sit right down

and keep your legs relaxed around Bob.'

My body jogs up and down as Bob trots in the shallow waters.

As the cold waters splash up and hit me I squeal, and Moon-Star laughs.

'Shh, Bee,' he says, as my squealing echoes round the trees.

Then I start to enjoy the feel of the waters' icy cold fingers tickling me and it makes me laugh too.

'Right, Bee, you are ready to go in. Grab hold of Bob's mane.'

And slowly, Moon-Star wades into the middle of the pool. As the waters get deeper, he starts to swim.

Bob follows him and, as the front part of his body goes down in the water, I am lifted up. I hardly dare breathe. I grip Bob's mane, but my body is floating and the waters aren't pulling me down. Bob and Moon-Star are keeping me safe, and as I relax, I begin to notice how the moon's rays are reflecting in the water surrounding Moon-Star.

He laughs, splashing his fingers in the dark, silvery water.

'Come on, Bee, reach for the moon's reflection; reach for its light. Come on, Bee . . . Let go and reach! I'll catch you.'

'I can't,' I say.

'You can. Remember the pact. You can't break it.'

He's right. I take a deep breath and let go of Bob's reins and mane with one hand, then the other, and *splash* – I'm kicking my legs. One, two, three. I'm swimming to the moon! My fingers are bathed in silver as I reach for its reflection.

Moon-Star grabs me and hugs me in the water. 'You've done it, Bee! You swam three strokes.'

Bob splashes past us and makes his way to the shallow bit, then up to the bank. He shakes his coat and the water drops sparkle off him in the night air.

Moon-Star lets go and swims a few strokes ahead of me. I doggy-paddle like crazy towards him then he does it again and again and again. He holds his arms out and I swim four strokes to him, then five, then six, then seven, till my toes touch the muddy river bottom and safety. I can't believe I did it!

I shiver as I get out of the water and run across the grassy bank to the towels.

I throw two to Moon-Star.

'One for you, and one for Bob,' I say.

Moon-Star laughs. 'Thanks.'

I run back under the willow tree to get changed and notice my inhaler is lying on the grass. I haven't used it once.

After I've got dressed, I peep out between the willow branches. Moon-Star is whispering to Bob as he rubs him with the towel, telling him secrets. I wonder what he is saying.

He looks up at me and winks.

I shiver again.

'We need to warm up,' I say, as an idea pops into my brain.

'Let's run – in the shapes of letters,' I say, shivering.

And we run a B and E and another E for BEE and then we spell out MOON and STAR and BOB who trots after us, neighing, loving the game.

Then Bob rolls on the grassy bank and we roll too until he stops and we lie there, resting our heads on Bob, looking up at the stars. I point to the largest, twinkliest one. 'That's Great-Gran Beatrix,' I say.

'You miss her, don't ya,' says Moon-Star, and he reaches out to link my thumb with his.

'Yes,' I say, and I feel as if I will choke. I swallow and squash back the tears.

We lie there in silence until I say, 'Do you miss your mum? What's Daisy like?'

Moon-Star doesn't say anything for a moment and all I can hear is the sound of my heart pounding. When Moon-Star eventually speaks, his voice shakes.

'You know in the morning dew, when the snail trails glisten and there's shimmering cobwebs clinging to things?'

I nod.

'Well Daisy, she's like a cobweb, blown away in the wind, delicate and fragile and so, so beautiful but she won't cling to nothing or nobody. A wisp of the wind and she's off. And she feels things so intense, it scrambles with my head. She laughs so much she cries and she loves so much she hates, and I try, I really do try, but sometimes she's just too much. And then they come, those people, and say I can't live with her no more and Gran comes and says, "*Ain't no one taking my grandson anywhere and I will see he gets book learning.*"'

I grab the whole of his hand and squeeze it hard.

'You know if ever I do have to go away . . .' says Moon-Star.

'Don't,' I say before I can stop myself.

'Bee, if ever I do, just look up at the moon and know you always have a friend on this planet.'

17

As the days and weeks start to tick nearer and nearer to the sponsored swim, I do my very best not to think about it. Every time the fear grips me, I close my eyes and count to ten.

I sit next to Moon-Star every day – teaching him letters under the desk and trying to do my own lessons at the same time.

Mrs Partridge has given him some one-to-one time but it's like she doesn't expect anything of him, like she's given up. I can see it in the looks she gives him.

'She ain't a good teacher like you is, Bee,' says Moon-Star. 'I prefer doing my book learning with you.'

But I still see the panic in his eyes. Then his

body judders and he gets up and paces round the class with wildness in his legs.

The whispering goes on, 'They should be moved on, moved on, moved on,' but Moon-Star and I don't listen.

'Look out of the window,' I tell him. 'Think of Bob enjoying Mr Gregory's grass. Think of you, me and Bob running through the fields.'

Moon-Star shuts his eyes and smiles and I see the stress dance out of his body, just for a moment.

I wish Mrs Partridge would realise how brave Moon-Star is, just for sitting behind a desk. But she just doesn't get it, like most grown-ups don't.

I've had to tell my mum that Chrystal and I are friends again, so she thinks I am watching her at clarinet, or gymnastics, or ballet or tap-dancing classes, when really I'm with Moon-Star.

He taps on my bedroom window every evening and we climb down to the garden and over the fence to where Bob is waiting for us in the fields at the back of the houses in Duck Street. I always wear my bowler hat and red feather boa, and Moon-Star wears my trilby with the feather on it. We both have dazzling style.

I love riding through the trees on Bob. We always reach up to the Promise Tree, trailing our fingers through its tickling leaves and drawing letters in the sky. Sometimes, when we pass the hives, the bees land on my red feather boa and I keep my body as still as can be until they fly away again. Slowly, I feel my legs and arms tingling with strength.

One evening, we reach our pool but Bob does not stop.

'Where are we going?' I say.

'You'll see,' says Moon-Star, and we cut through fields and quieter country paths till we are at the back of Ashton Leisure Complex. THE SWIMMING POOL FOR THE SPONSORED SWIM.

'It's almost time for them to shut up for the night,' says Moon-Star. 'We'll wait.'

'We can't go in when it's closed,' I say.

'Watch me,' says Moon-Star.

He tethers Bob to a fence and we hide in the bushes. A warm breeze ruffles our hair as we peep through the twigs and watch as everyone leaves. I can't decide if I feel more scared of swimming, or breaking into the pool when we really, really shouldn't.

'Now,' says Moon-Star, and he runs to the leisure centre wall. I have no choice but to follow him. He gives me a leg up to a window ledge. My legs and arms are flapping everywhere and I'm struggling to pull myself up, so I pretend I am in a film, playing top-secret spy Mademoiselle Le Bee, saving the world from war. And somehow, I manage to haul myself up on to the ledge. Moon-Star appears beside me.

We peek through the window and there's Chrystal! She's having a private diving lesson. Bryony, her muscly personal trainer, stands by the side of the pool in white shorts and a T-shirt, yelling, 'Stretch your legs, Chrystal!' 'That's more like it, Chrystal!' 'Do it again, Chrystal!'

while Chrystal somersaults, twists and backflips into the pool again and again and again.

Moon-Star does a hushed whistle under his breath, 'She's good.'

I nod, feeling a bee sting of jealousy.

Eventually, Chrystal climbs out of the pool, Bryony holds a towel out for her and they disappear into the changing room. The lights are turned off as they go. The pool is now closed for the night.

'They never shut this window properly,' whispers Moon-Star and he pushes it open, throws our towels through the gap and helps me climb through.

I can just reach a bench running underneath the window with my toes.

Moon-Star scrambles through after me.

I wriggle out of my onesie; my swimming costume is underneath. Moon-Star strips down to his shorts. I walk round the edge of the pool. The water looks eerie in the darkened room. Gazing up at the gallery, my heart stops. In four days' time, it will be filled with people watching

me, and even though I'm stronger, I still can't
– won't – put my head underwater and I can
only swim a few splashes. I haven't got any
sponsors and . . . and . . . and . . .

'Get in,' says Moon-Star, turning up the
lights a tiny bit. He manages to force open a
cupboard and throws a float into the deep end.
He grabs all our stuff and pushes it into the
cupboard, kicking the door shut.

'Go on, Bee.'

I get into the pool, one step at a time. The
smell of chlorine makes my nose tingle. The
cold water slowly creeps up my body as I climb
down the stairs until my feet reach the bottom.

Moon-Star lowers himself in next to me with
a little splash.

'Right then, we're going to go for a width,'
Moon-Star says, walking backwards. I doggy-
paddle towards him and reach out for his hand,
but he steps backwards again. I'm trying and
trying but every time I nearly reach him he
steps back. I start to feel cross, but Moon-Star
just laughs and ducks under the water.

Suddenly, I touch the side of the swimming pool. I've done it! I've actually swum a width, without arm floats!

Moon-Star erupts like a whale through the surface of the water.

'I knew you could do it, Bee.' We high-five then hold on to the side, laughing, kicking our legs, spelling 'Moon-Star' and 'Bee' with our toes.

Then we hear a voice call out, 'My bracelet – I must have left it.'

It's Chrystal! Before I even have time to think, I have taken a big breath and ducked underwater. Moon-Star is under too, cheeks puffed out, eyes wide, hair outstretched like a lion's mane, waving in the water. He puts his finger to his lips.

When my lungs feel like they're about to pop I rise to the top, spluttering, just in time to see the changing-room door swing back as Chrystal leaves. A second earlier and she would have caught us.

Moon-Star bursts out of the water next to me.

He still has his finger over his lips as a giggle splutters out of my mouth.

We wait till we hear the sound of footsteps over gravel and a car starting up.

'I did it,' I say. 'I actually held my head underwater!'

Moon-Star grins. 'So you did.'

He swims after the float. 'Here you go,' he says, but keeps hold of it. 'Now you're going to do a length.'

I keep stretching for the float but again Moon-Star tricks me, holding it just out of reach.

'Please, Moon-Star . . .'

I can't go on. I need to stop. *Please*.

'Look,' he says, pointing ahead of him.

It's dark outside now, and the moon is shining through the window, reflecting in the water.

'Reach for the moon,' he says. 'Swim to the moon, Bee!'

So I do. My legs are heavy, my arms are aching, but I keep swimming until I touch the end of the pool.

MY VERY FIRST LENGTH!

18

Moon-Star hauls me out of the pool.

'I think we'd better get out of here,' he says. 'We've chanced our luck enough.'

I nod, and head to the cupboard for our things. I grab my inhaler and take a puff.

We quickly pull our clothes on over our wet swimming costumes, scramble out of the window, run over the grass and climb on to Bob. We're both shivering, so I wrap the feather boa around us for warmth. Then through the woods we go, laughing, chatting, celebrating my length.

The heat from Bob's body warms me up. He prances and snorts and trots.

'Bob's saying he's real proud of you,'

Moon-Star tells me.

I laugh, happy bubbles fizzing in my brain. Who needs Chrystal Kelly when I have the best friends in the world: Moon-Star and Bob.

'Shhh,' says Moon-Star suddenly. 'What's that?'

There are voices.

Strange white flecks of something tumble along the ground towards us. Bob sniffs them. They look like snow but they can't be . . . It's summer!

Slowly, we ride forward, the only sound the cracking of twigs under Bob's hooves.

More strange speckles of white.

Then laughter.

'Are we ready to go?' says a man's voice.

'Nearly, I just need to brush my hair!' It sounds like Chrystal.

'Quickly, quickly,' snaps the man's voice.

We creep forward. I pull on the reins to stop Bob behind an oak tree with a huge trunk. Moon-Star leans over my shoulder and we peep through the branches.

I choke back a gasp.

Mayor Kelly is standing in front of us, wearing a long brown robe. On his head he's got a tea towel with one of Chrystal's headbands around it, but he's still wearing his golden mayor's livery collar round his neck.

Mrs Kelly is next to him, in a long blue dress and matching tea towel. I have to bite on my lip really hard to stop a naughty giggle rising as I realise that they are dressed as Mary and Joseph from the Nativity story! Only, I don't think Joseph had a fat belly and Mary definitely didn't wear false eyelashes.

They look so silly. My giggle rises higher, nearly choking me, as I notice Burt and Alfie, Mayor Kelly's stooges, waving hoses attached to a machine, out of which is pouring fake snow.

Standing on wobbly ballet pointe, dressed as an angel with a halo hovering over her blonde curls, is Chrystal. She's wearing her most sickening, simpering smile and is holding Mitzi the chihuahua, who is also dressed as an angel with wings and a little halo.

Then my heart jolts. In the crib is little Daniel. He's lying in the straw, wrapped in a blanket, and he looks just perfect as baby Jesus.

A bearded photographer is fixing a camera to a tripod.

'What are they doing?' whispers Moon-Star.

I twist round on Bob. 'It's for their Christmas card,' I hiss in Moon-Star's ear. 'They do a picture every year. Last year it was Santa's grotto. Chrystal and Mitzi wore matching pixie hats.'

Moon-Star snorts with laughter and my giggle explodes, so we stuff our fists in our mouths, tears pouring down our faces. But then Bob properly gives us away. He spots the straw in the manger and charges forward, sending fairy lights and fake snow flying everywhere. My heart catapults into my mouth as Moon-Star topples off into a bush. I pull back on Bob's reins as much as I can.

'No, Bob! NO!' I shout.

But he's on a mission. He's seen food! He reaches the manger and halts so suddenly I am flung forward. I wrap my arms around his neck, just about managing to stay on his back.

Bob gives Daniel a lick. I freeze, but Daniel giggles and grabs Bob's mane in his fist. I know Bob wouldn't mean to hurt him, but he's a horse and he's so big and Daniel's tiny. I slide off Bob and scoop Daniel up into my arms just as Bob takes a huge mouthful of straw, knocks the manger over and stands on it.

As the sound of splintering wood hits my ears, Chrystal and Mrs Kelly scream. Bob rears in fear.

'I'VE GOT DANIEL!' I shout, hugging him to me.

Then everything happens at once.

Bob, still spooked, rears again. Moon-Star appears, covered in twigs and fake snow, holding out his hand to calm his horse. Mayor Kelly runs towards Bob but trips on his own robe and falls backwards on to his fat bottom, while Mrs Kelly runs round and round in circles, wailing, 'Our Christmas card! Our beautiful Christmas card is ruined!'

The bearded photographer quickly packs up his equipment, muttering to himself.

Mitzi jumps down from Chrystal's arms and runs up and down yapping, so Moon-Star picks up the little dog and untangles her from the angel costume. He waves the angel wings in the air, shouting, 'FREEDOM FOR MITZI.'

I don't know where to look, then I hear Chrystal yelling as she charges towards me.

'BEE EDWARDS, I HATE YOU AND YOUR SMELLY, DIRTY, SCRUFFY BOYFRIEND!'

My blood boils. 'DON'T YOU DARE SAY THOSE THINGS ABOUT MOON-STAR!' I yell back. 'He's a far better friend than you ever were.'

'Give me my brother back.' Chrystal is right in front of me now. 'You will never touch him again,' she hisses, snatching him from my arms.

My heart breaks right then.

'Let's get out of here,' says Moon-Star, putting Mitzi down and hauling me back towards Bob.

'We never meant to hurt you,' says

Moon-Star as we clamber on to Bob's back. 'Bob's a horse – he saw food and he was hungry. We never meant you no harm. Come on, boy – home.'

Mayor Kelly's voice comes booming after us, 'The sooner you people move on, the better.'

I dig really, really, deep so I won't cry, and I turn round and give Moon-Star my very best smile, a smile that says Moon-Star and Bee shall never be parted.

Moon-Star doesn't smile back.

19

I wake with an uneasy tangle in my heart. As I trace the honeybees' wings on the wall with my fingers, everything that happened yesterday starts to kick back into my memory. I peel off the queen bee and hold her in the palm of my hand.

'*The sooner you people move on, the better.*' Mayor Kelly's words stab my brain.

Supposing Moon-Star's not at school; supposing he and Old Alice . . .

I get ready for school, desperately hoping Moon-Star will be there.

Through the crack in the dining-room door I can see Dad reading the paper and eating toast and tea.

I creep past.

'Bee,' calls Dad. He's seen me.

'Oh, morning, Dad,' I say, digging deep for my very best *I totally honestly did not see you there* face.

'Mum tells me you and the mayor's daughter have made up. You girls and your silly little squabbles, eh!' He actually pats me on the head as if I'm a dog.

No words come. Silly little squabbles! My own dad doesn't know the first thing about my life. Chrystal was my best friend in the whole world till the day of the double-double-dare and he doesn't even care that she's now a horrible bully – all he cares about is getting in with the mayor. He makes me sick.

Act, a voice inside my head tells me. *Act your heart out, like Marilyn would. If he thinks you are with Chrystal, he won't suspect that you're with Moon-Star.*

'Thank you, Dad,' I manage. 'Like Mum told you, we've made up our silly little quarrel, and I am having lots of fun with Chrystal and watching her do her many, many activities. It is so nice to see you. Enjoy your breakfast.'

Marilyn would be proud!

Mum is in the kitchen, cleaning her paintbrushes. The sponsor form on the fridge taunts me. Then I see Mum's added her name.

Mum: £3.00 a length

'Oh, you've sponsored me! Thanks, Mum,' I say.

'Even if you just swim a few splashes, I'll be so proud. And so would your great-gran be if she were here.'

I quickly busy myself, shoving the sponsor form in my bag – number one, so I don't have to look at it every time I come into the kitchen and, number two, so Mum can't see that my eyes are prickling.

But Mum's not fooled. She gives me a hug. 'It takes more courage to attempt the things we can't do, than to achieve in things we can,' she says. 'Now, what would you like for breakfast?'

'No time, sorry.'

I run straight out of the door, shutting my

eyes, as I always do. I swear I can feel the old people watching me from the Rise and Shine.

I do my twenty-five hops over the bridge without wobbling even once.

When I reach the clearing, Old Alice is sitting on the steps of the wagon, smoking her pipe.

'Moon-Star's restless,' she tells me. 'He's taken off for a gallop on Bob. Best to leave him when he's vexed. He'll see you at school I'm sure, Bee.'

So I trudge on to school alone.

I tumble through the school gates a short while later, tripping on the strap of my bag.

I search for Moon-Star. I can't see him. The elephant climbs on to my chest as I spot Chrystal standing in the middle of a crowd of girls. I wheeze and hurriedly take a puff of my inhaler.

Chrystal turns round and her eyes laser spite-swords into mine. I stare back – she's not going to win, not this time.

Chrystal turns away and waves a glittery lilac folder in the air.

'I've got lots of sponsors. My dad took it to a

meeting of all his business associates in town and every single one of them said it was a pleasure to sponsor me. Bryony says it's very important for me to conserve my energy, so I am just going to swim the two lengths required so I don't tire myself out for the dance extravaganza afterwards. This way, I can raise lots of money for the old people and also give them a lovely dance show to remember. It's very important we all do our bit. Wouldn't you agree, Bee?' She slings that last bit over her shoulder to me. 'But of course, you don't have to worry about the dance extravaganza cos you're not in it!' She turns and laughs at me, her hands on her hips. 'How many sponsors have you got, Bee? Go on – show me.'

'No,' I say, but Chrystal opens my bag and pulls my form out anyway. 'Oh my . . . an "X". Was that from one of your traveller friends who can't even write? Oh and your mum! Two sponsors, Bee . . . My form is full! Oh, but I forgot, you can't even swim, so your TWO sponsors won't have to pay you any money anyway!'

Everyone laughs.

'Three,' says a voice. I turn. Moon-Star is walking towards us. 'She has three sponsors.'

He grabs a pen from my pencil case and snatches the form from Chrystal. Then he writes very slowly, mouthing each letter as he forms it.

MOON-STAR HIGGINS £2.00

My heart bursts with pride. This is one of my all-time best moments in my life. He hands me back my form and we link thumbs as we walk into the classroom.

'You've got four sponsors actually, cos Bob's teeth marks are his signature,' whispers Moon-Star, pointing to the chewed corner.

I laugh. It starts to rain but I don't care.

'Look, Moon-Star, a rainbow,' I say, pointing to the beautiful colours splashed across the sky above us.

I feel as if I can do anything.

I paint a rainbow in art that afternoon. Moon-Star's picture is the best in the class, as always. He's drawing a picture of the Promise Tree and the beehives and me and him reaching up into its branches. I can hear Chrystal in the background as I paint in the red arc in my rainbow, running from desk to desk, whispering things.

The words 'Traveller . . . Dirty . . . Move on . . .' reach my ears but I'm trying to block them out. I'm not going to let Chrystal burst my happy bubble.

I look at Moon-Star, but he's so lost in his new painting of a camper van with daisies painted on it and a blonde lady with dancing skirts swirling, he doesn't hear the poisonous whispers. I throw myself back into my art, starting a second painting of the little grey kitten asleep on Old Alice's bed.

Moon-Star links thumbs with me all the way home from school, but when we reach the clearing in the woods we find Old Alice sitting on the wagon steps with her head in her hands.

'Oh, Moon-Star,' she says, 'I don't know what's to become of us. They've turned off our water supply!'

My happy bubble bursts.

20

Moon-Star sits next to Old Alice on the wagon steps and puts his arm around her.

'We've only got a tiny bit of rainwater,' Old Alice says, nodding to a bucket by the wagon steps.

'They can't do this to you, they just can't,' I say.

I run to the tap and turn it on and off a few times, just to make sure Old Alice isn't mistaken, but not a drop of water comes out.

No one can survive without water. It's not possible. I'll have to get them some . . .

'Moon-Star, wait here. I'll be back.' I have a plan.

I stumble through the trees, hop twenty-five times over the bridge without a single wobble and run as fast as I ever have. My legs and arms are flapping in all directions, but I don't care.

Chrystal is sitting in her usual spot in the tree in her garden, legs dangling from the branch. She laughs as I run past, and waves a piece of paper in the air.

'I was just counting all my sponsors, Bee. Going to wear arm floats in the sponsored swim, are you?'

Not bothering to answer back, I just run . . . run . . . run.

A stitch stabs in my side just as I'm nearing my house, and a wheeze escapes. I dig around in my bag for my inhaler and take a puff, staggering the last few steps home. It's a relief to see that Dad's car isn't there yet. I just need Mum.

I hammer on the door. Mum opens it.

'Mum,' I say, gasping. 'Please! You've got to help!'

'Bee, what's happened? Are you OK?'

I try to speak. I take a puff of my inhaler and try again.

'Mu—'

'Where's Chrystal?' she butts in. 'I thought you were with her?'

I take a deep breath and it all comes spilling out of me. 'Mum, please. I'm not . . . with Chrystal. I'm never with Chrystal. I hate Chrystal . . . Kelly. It's Moon-Star and Old Alice – their . . . water's been turned off. Please . . . Mum, they need drinking water or . . . they'll die and there's Bob the horse and the kitten and, well, all the . . . cats and even the bees need water cos if the flowers die there'll be no nectar . . . and . . . and . . .'

Mum pulls me inside. 'They can't leave an old lady without any water. That's not right. We'll take some to her.'

I fling my arms round Mum. 'I knew you'd understand.'

Mum has a sparkle in her eye as she starts pulling bottles out of the recycling bin. I run to the garden shed and find some of the giant plastic bottles that Mum saves to mix paint in. I dump them in the kitchen then speed back to the garden shed for the wheelbarrow.

Mum boils kettles to sterilise the bottles,

then we fill them with drinking water from the tap. We load up the wheelbarrow and head out to the road, the Russian-doll houses getting bigger and bigger as we walk.

Mum and I take turns. It's heavy work.

Relief floods me from top to toe as I see Chrystal's tree is now empty, but the relief soon vanishes when we reach the road over the crooked bridge. Mum takes the wheelbarrow, and I hop behind her, counting.

'One, two, three.'

'What are you doing, Bee?' Mum asks.

'Nothing special, Mum,' I lie.

'Four, five, six.'

A car speeds past us and beeps, making me lose my place. Mum wobbles with the barrow, so I grab hold of one of the handles and we push it together to the end of the bridge. I count in my head and do a kind of one-footed tap as we go.

The sound of a hammer hitting wood echoes through the branches as we approach.

'Quick, Mum,' I say, grabbing both the handles. 'Something's wrong, I know it. Hurry!'

Sweat pours down my face and my arms ache as we reach the clearing. But there's a team of workmen blocking our way. They're erecting an enormous mesh wire fence with cruel-looking barbed spikes running along the top. Burt and Alfie are knocking wooden posts into the ground to support the fence.

They're building a prison for Moon-Star and Old Alice!

'NOOOO!' I scream. 'WHAT ARE YOU DOING?'

'YOU SHOULD BE ASHAMED OF YOURSELVES! IT'S AN OLD LADY AND A CHILD IN THERE! LET US THROUGH, NOW!' Mum yells. She means business.

I recognise some of the men as dads of pupils from my school. I hear a few mutterings about travellers and moving on, but none of them can look us in the eye as they step aside to let us through.

'Mum, you are amazing,' I whisper. 'Great-Gran Beatrix would say you're a unique individual.'

Mum winks at me as we make our way into the clearing.

Moon-Star is slumped on the wagon steps, then he looks up, sees us and runs to help.

We start unloading the bottles of water from the barrow. I fill Bob's bucket and he trots up and starts slurping. Water splashes everywhere.

'This is my mum,' I say to Moon-Star.

'Hello,' she says with a smile. 'This should keep you going for a bit.'

Old Alice comes down the wagon steps. 'Thank ye for the water,' she says. 'We're much obliged.'

Moon-Star nods at Mum, hands in pockets, then he scuffs his foot in the ground, sending clouds of dust towards the fence.

Burt and Alfie and the team of men continue to unroll the barbed wire fence, attaching it to wooden posts along the perimeter of the woods.

Any moment now we will be trapped inside.

'Come away,' says Mum, 'quick.'

'I can't, Mum,' I say. 'These are my friends.'

'Go,' says Moon-Star gruffly, a harsh look on his face I've not seen before. 'This is our fight, not yours. Go home to your *house*.'

I feel as if my heart has been stung by a bee.

Then Mum takes my hand and pulls me through the gap in the wire, just before it's sealed off.

I turn and watch as Moon-Star and Old Alice slowly climb the steps and disappear into the red wagon.

I can't sleep; I lie in bed worrying, wondering how long the fence is. Supposing it takes Moon-Star so long to get to school that he doesn't bother coming any more? What about the pact?

I turn on my yellow bedside lamp. Judy and Marilyn smile down at me from the film-star wall. My bumblebee alarm clock says it's two o'clock in the morning, but I know that I have to go now, this minute, to see Moon-Star. I pull on jeans and a big green jumper and my DMs and reach for the trilby that Moon-Star always wears, then I creep down the stairs and out of the front door.

There are some lights still on in the Rise and Shine Happy Care Home for Older People. A curtain twitches and Matilda, who used to be a concert pianist, peers out into the dark. I duck down so she doesn't see me, then the curtain closes and I hear 'We're Off to See the Wizard' being played on her grand piano. I swallow, take a deep breath and carry on walking down the deserted street. I know I would be in the biggest trouble of my life if Mum and Dad knew I was out at two in the morning, but I have to get to Moon-Star.

I hop over the crooked bridge, my heart hammering, trying to ignore the dark waters as they gurgle below.

An owl hoots. I freeze. My breath shatters.

The elephant lurks behind every tree, their twisty shadows dark against the nearly full moon.

I grope for my inhaler in my jeans pocket and take a puff. The elephant runs off through the forest.

'Don't be silly, Bee,' I say out loud, 'be brave and walk, like Dorothy does in the Haunted Forest.'

So I stagger forward, my jumper and hair snatching at the twigs. There's a crackling sound, and behind the barbed-wire fence I see a bonfire of beautiful yellow and orange flames, reaching towards the moon. The red wagon, lit up in the reflection of the flames, is flickering and mystical. Then I hear bells tinkling and a lady with daisies woven into her long wavy blonde hair spins into view.

She's twirling, her golden skirts swishing round, and she's wearing silver bells around her ankles. A nose stud catches the light, and she laughs and it's so beautiful, like a song of the night that I swear is making the leaves in the trees rustle. She's clapping her hands, bewitching me, and my feet start twitching and itching to dance.

A camper van painted with daisies is parked up next to the red wagon. Moon-Star is sitting on the wagon's steps. He sees me and runs up to the wire fence. I push my thumb through a hole and Moon-Star links it with his.

We stand there in the moonlight, then Moon-Star says, 'She's come . . . my ma.'

And I love the twirling lady with the blonde hair and daisies, who named her son Moon-Star.

'Can I get in?' I ask.

'Well, they've fenced in the whole clearing, and the beehives and the Promise Tree, so there's just a tunnel of wire leading to the road out of here. But there's a gap I've made they don't know about, a'fore you get to the end of the tunnel. You oughta be able to squeeze through.'

'At least the bees can fly over the fence,' I say, and press my hand against the wire.

'They can't stop the bees,' says Moon-Star, and he presses his hand against mine through the fence.

We walk along, our hands touching through the wire till they can touch no more, because we've reached a clump of trees blocking the way.

'Now, run, Bee,' says Moon-Star. 'I'll be waiting for ya.'

I sprint through the twisted, snarled trees, and suddenly I can't see him any more. My arms slash through the night air, reaching – reaching for Moon-Star.

I pass the sleeping bees in their hives and the Promise Tree, the stars peeping between its branches.

Our secret pool glints in the dark to the right of me.

'Bee, Bee, Bee,' I hear him calling me.

'I'm here,' I cry.

Moon-Star steps out from behind a tree. He links my thumb in his and helps me through the gap in the wire.

We make our way through the trees towards the fire.

'Come, child, dance,' says Daisy, drawing me towards her. 'They try to imprison us but they have failed – we are free spirits. Come, shake out your pretty red hair in the moonlight.'

Old Alice comes to greet me. 'Couldn't sleep, eh, little one?' she says, brushing my cheek with her finger. 'But you know that running around in the dark on your own isn't the finest idea, don't you? We don't need no more trouble bringing to our door.'

'Sorry, Old Alice, I didn't think. I just . . .'

'Don't worry your head. You're here now,' she says, then disappears into her wagon and brings out something white and shimmery and hands it to me. I shake it out and gasp – it's a white dress with swirly-swirly skirts, just like Marilyn Monroe's. I run to hug the old lady, a tear already splashing down my cheek.

'How, Old Alice? How did you know?'

'Do you think Old Alice don't see you walking all fancy like Marilyn Monroe, when ye think no one's looking? Do you think Moon-Star didn't tell me about your wall of film stars? Old Alice knows everything. I made it for you in thanks for Moon-Star doing his book learning.'

She whispers in my ear, 'I've stitched the neckline higher than Marilyn's to hide your modesty. You're not a woman yet. Though you'll be one soon enough.' She winks at me.

I dash into the wagon, wriggle out of my clothes and into the shimmy-shimmy dress. It falls over me like silky waves over a beach.

I walk out of the wagon. Moon-Star smiles and Daisy clasps my hand and we twist and twirl. And I don't feel all elbows and knees. I feel magical. Old Alice brings out a harmonica and plays a tune that tells of lands and castles far away. Moon-Star claps, then when I think we can dance no more he brings a big square board from inside the camper van. He has these black shiny shoes on his feet which glisten in the firelight, and he stands on the board and starts to do steps on it, his feet going *clickety-clack*, faster and faster, like his shiny shoes are on fire.

When he flops down for a rest, I plonk myself on the ground beside him.

'Where did you learn to dance like that?'

''Tis Gypsy step dancing. My friend Romany Joe, he showed me the steps at Appleby Fair. He taught me more steps every year, till I had 'em to perfection.'

'Joe – he's who you got Bob from, right?' I remembered.

'Yes, Bee. Joe's family are horse dealers. Me and Ma saw Joe racing Bob down the flash and he galloped so fast he were flying, his white tail and mane all wild in the wind.'

Daisy claps her hands, dancing up to us. 'I knew he was the horse for my Moon-Star,' she says. Then she's off again, twirling round and round the fire.

'Getting Bob is the best thing I ever done,' Moon-Star says. 'He's the only steady thing I got when I'm on the road with my ma. Bob's my family. Day I got him, Joe took him for cleansing in the River Eden, before he were sold to me – it's tradition, see. As Bob splashes up the riverbank, I looks at Joe and pulls a face and he pulls a face back at me and we have a muck-about fight and Bob charges through us and Joe's ma, Lala, shouts at us to stop messing as we're flustering the horse. Then I see her watching my ma, Daisy, who's laughing higher and higher and running about in circles like her feet won't stop – then Daisy's tears start to fall and Lala, she won't rest till she calms my ma and feeds us both stew and bread.'

I give Moon-Star's arm a quick squeeze cos I've just realised that it's Moon-Star who's the grown-up and Daisy's the child and that must be hard, *really hard*, for Moon-Star. I look into the fire till my eyes sting, thinking that I'm lucky to have my mum.

After a bit I say, 'Joe's mum sounds like a kind lady.'

Moon-Star nods his head.

'She looked out for us, Lala did. When Appleby was over and they were ready to hit the road, she says to me, "Moon-Star, makes sure you come next year. I just need to see how things are with you," and then she tapped her heart and gave me a loaf of bread to take back to the Daisymobile.'

I want so badly to hug Moon-Star's sadness away but I can't, so I shuffle my bottom a little closer to him.

'Me and Ma travels round the country to festivals and horse fairs and we visit Appleby every year to see Joe.'

'You must come with me – all of you,' says Daisy, twirling towards us, clapping her hands, her laughter all silvery. 'Come into the Daisymobile. Come . . . Come round the world, the adventures we shall have – come with Daisy.'

It was like she was enchanting me with magic. I could feel my feet itching to travel in the Daisymobile. Me and Moon-Star, for ever and ever, exploring hills and villages and riding Bob in the forest. No Dad to hurt my feelings, no Chrystal, no school.

And Daisy claps her hands and clicks her fingers and her laughter gets higher and higher till it turns into a waterfall of sparkly tears. Moon-Star rushes to put his arms around her.

'The girl and Moon-Star are staying here,' says Old Alice firmly. 'They've got book learning to do.'

'Ma, come with us,' says Daisy, her mood suddenly dark as the night sky.

'I can't, Daisy,' Old Alice replies. 'How many times do I have to say it?'

'You can't stay here, Ma, it's a prison. There's no water; they'll get you in the end.'

'I'm staying here for the bees and for Moon-Star to do his book learning, you know that, Daisy.'

'We can't be here without water,' says Moon-Star, 'trapped like animals.'

Dread crawls up my spine. Moon-Star's going to leave me.

'No, please,' I say, 'I'll bring you water every day.'

'We wants our own water,' says Moon-Star.

'But the pact,' I say, panic rising, about to choke me.

'It's nearly done,' he says. 'I know some letters and you can swim, sorta.'

The bottom falls out of my world. He can't leave me.

'No!' I say. 'No, please. Old Alice, tell him!'

'Moon-Star,' says Old Alice, 'you know what will happen if you go. They'll come and get you and lock you away to do your learning. You're meant to go to school every day, not just when the mood takes you.'

Then she puts her hands on my shoulders and her eyes spark with warning. 'Child, get changed – 'tis time to go home. Go home, to your own people.'

21

I wait and wait in the playground the next morning, but there's no sign of Moon-Star. In assembly I keep turning to the door every time I hear a noise, hoping it's him, but it never is. Partridge keeps glaring and flapping her hands for me to face the front.

'We are all looking forward to the sponsored swim and dance gala the day after tomorrow,' Mr Gregory says.

I don't listen to one more word that's said. Sponsored swim . . . Moon-Star . . . sponsored swim . . . Moon-Star . . . keeps repeating like a drum beat in my brain.

Moon-Star's gone with Daisy and I'll never see him again. I feel sick. My old friend the elephant sits back in his favourite chair – my chest. I wheeze and take a sneaky puff of my inhaler.

As usual everyone pushes and shoves their way out of assembly. I'm too busy looking out for Moon-Star to pay attention to where I am going. Chrystal puts her foot out and sends me sprawling, just as I enter the classroom.

Everyone laughs. I scramble to my feet, hold my head up high and walk to my desk. I look at the empty space next to it.

'Where's your boyfriend?' hisses Chrystal from across the classroom. I shrug my shoulders.

'Shhh, Chrystal Saffron Kelly,' says Mrs Partridge. 'But yes – Bee, do you know where Moon-Star is today?'

'He's got a bad cold,' I lie and pretend to be answering the geography questions on rivers of the British Isles. The only rivers I'm interested in are ones I can splash in with Moon-Star and Bob.

The desk beside me remains empty. I keep looking at the classroom clock, cheering on the seconds until they eventually drag themselves over the finishing line, then I take the quickest way I can to Old Alice's clearing. I only slow as I pass the hives, so as not to scare the bees.

I sprint down the path and my heart stops.

The camper van has gone – there are just wheel marks in the grass and mud. I'm too late; he's left with his ma.

'Moon-Star,' I cry, up to the clouds. 'Moon-Star!'

He appears round the back of the wagon.

My heart soars.

'I thought I'd never see you again!' I cry and run to him, my arms reaching out for a hug. But Moon-Star turns on his heel and starts down the path towards the bees and the Promise Tree.

'Bee, I'm a traveller – travelling is what I do. You have to get that into yer head.'

My arms fall to my side and I follow him, my heart in my boots and my cheeks burning.

Old Alice is crouched, almost hidden, on the other side of the Promise Tree. She is leaning over a metal jug thing with bellows attached.

I watch as she sets to work lighting it with fuel and grass and woodchips, then gently pumps the bellows until smoke puffs out of the spout.

'I needs to check for pesky mites in the hive, see, but I don't want them bees to be cross and sting me,' says Old Alice. 'The smoke fools 'em that their hive's on fire and they need to find a new home, so they start guzzling all the honey till their little bellies are stuffed and they're too sluggish to sting.'

She looks up and nods to an old cardboard box on the grass beside her.

'Are you two going to stand there gawping, or are you going to make yourself useful and help Old Alice with a spot of beekeeping? Get yerself a suit.'

My heart flutters with joy. I've waited for this moment for ever.

'Gran, I don't need one,' Moon-Star swaggers. 'I can charm the bees, me.'

Old Alice looks up and her eyes spark at him. 'No suit – no bees. You'll do as I bid, Moon-Star Higgins. Both of you. If I'm an old fool bee-charmer who takes the risk, that's my lookout.'

I swear my breath stops. I am actually going to see inside a hive! I rummage in the cardboard box to find a suit and welly boots that look as if they'll fit.

Moon-Star steps into his suit over his jeans, but I've got a school skirt on so I duck behind the Promise Tree and wriggle into my PE shorts. Then I step into a suit, zip the hood on and look out through the net. We look like strange squashy spacemen.

Old Alice puffs some smoke into the doorway of the hive to stop the bees flying out. Then she slowly lifts the lid and gently prises off the inner cover with a metal tool. Inside is a row of frames, a bit like wooden picture frames but they are arranged vertically like the files in Dad's filing cabinet. It's a filing cabinet of bees.

I hold my breath as Old Alice gently lifts a frame out of the hive. It's covered in honeycomb and bees and glorious stickiness, and some of the hexagons are capped with beeswax, which means there's a baby bee growing inside.

And I'm not scared, not one little bit, not even when the buzzing gets louder and louder and some bees fly out. They zoom around me, drawing letters in the air, hovering in front of my lips and eyelashes. Stripy, beautiful, furry bees.

Moon-Star and I smile at each other through the dancing bees.

'They're doing a waggle dance to show the other bees where to find flowers,' says Moon-Star.

I look at the frame Old Alice is holding.

'That's right,' Old Alice says. 'See – this bee here is feeding nectar from her tongue to show how tasty it is, so the other bees will want to know where they can get some.'

I watch as the bees cluster round. Then the bee feeding the nectar starts a dance. First it wiggles in a straight line, then loops round to the right, wiggles in a straight line again, then loops round to the left. It's like a dance-off for bees.

'The direction she wiggles in shows how far from the sun the flowers lie,' says Old Alice. 'And if it's really sweet nectar, she'll wiggle her little bee behind even faster.'

I watch transfixed as they wiggle-waggle their bottoms. It's the most beautiful thing ever on planet earth, way better than Chrystal's dance moves. Then I glance up and Moon-Star is giving me that look that goes through my soul. I feel my cheeks burn and quickly look back at the bees.

Old Alice chuckles. 'See how they're all competing with each other, little devils. They want to show that the nectar they've found is the sweetest. 'Tis the ancient dance of the honeybee. A hundred and fifty million years they've been doing this dance. Longer than we humans have been walking around.'

Old Alice gently lifts the rest of the frames, one at a time, to check for mites, then she closes the hive. They are all clear.

As I slowly walk away from the hive some bees follow me. But they take one look at my boring grey school skirt on the ground and leave to seek brightly coloured flowers.

I get changed, my head still in the magical

world of the bees' waggle dance.

'Get a wriggle on, Bee, tea's ready,' yells Moon-Star.

Old Alice has made bread and honey and chocolate cake and I'm starving but suddenly feel full of sadness that this won't last for ever. As I sit down, the little grey kitten wanders into the wagon and climbs on to my lap.

'Out,' says Old Alice, picking him off my knee and shooing him down the steps of the wagon. 'We're eating, little one.'

She closes the bottom part of the wagon door, leaving the top open. But while she's busy cutting the cake, the kitten climbs back in through the window and jumps straight on to my knee again.

'How's that sponsor form coming along?' Old Alice asks.

I shrug my shoulders.

'Has your da sponsored you?' she says.

'Nope,' I answer.

'Well, have you asked him? Don't ask, don't get . . .' she says.

Then something makes the hairs on the back of my neck stand on end. I whip my head round and see Burt and Alfie staring at us through the open wagon door.

I scream.

'Give 'em the letter, Alf,' growls Burt.

Alfie throws a letter into the wagon. It sails through the air and lands on the floor.

Moon-Star scoops it up as the men turn their backs and go.

'Would you read it for us, Bee?' asks Old Alice.

I rip open the letter and stare at the words in horror.

'It's a letter of eviction,' I say. 'They're going to make you leave. It says here that the mayor has given you three days to vacate the clearing because they are going to build houses in the woods.'

BANG! Something hits the side of the wagon.

I jump and the little kitten hisses, leaps off my knee and runs under the table.

Bob neighs and I hear the pounding of hooves. It sounds like he's galloping round the clearing.

THUD! That's the sound of the wagon being kicked.

Moon-Star jumps up, his face twisted with anger. Old Alice holds him back.

Then the wagon starts to rock. We grab on to each other. Crockery slips and slides. Two of Moon-Star's beautiful bowls crash to the ground, the dragons smashing into a thousand pieces. I reach for the chocolate cake as it slides to the edge of the table. The kitten is still hissing.

'WE WANT YOU GONE! DO YOU HEAR?' shouts Burt.

Then the rocking stops and we sit there in silence as the men's voices get fainter and fainter as they walk away chatting as if nothing has happened, till we can't hear them any more.

'I'm not easy with you being here, Bee,' says Old Alice. 'This is our fight, not yours. Run now, home to your ma and da. RUN!'

I don't want to, but I do what she says. I run.

22

It's getting dark. I smack into the fence. In my panic, I had forgotten it was there. I follow it to the gap Moon-Star made, then squeeze through, turning back on myself to run along the free side. As I pass the wagon, all I can see is Bob, standing under a tree and dozing. The wagon door is shut.

I reach the crooked bridge and begin to hop.

1, 2, 3, 4, 5, 6, 7, 8, 9, 10, 11, 12, 13, 14, 15, 16, 17, 18, 19, 20, 21, 22, 23, 24, 25.

I don't even notice as I cross the bridge without a single wobble, then I pound down the road, my head spinning. Life without Moon-Star . . . without Moon-Star . . . without Moon-Star.

I want to tell my mum about the eviction

letter, but Dad's car is outside the house.

I let myself in.

'You're late,' he calls from the dining room.

'Sorry,' I call back, trying not to sound wheezy. I take a quick puff of my inhaler. 'Got talking to Linford. Everyone at the Rise and Shine is excited about the swim.'

That's a terrible lie. I say a thousand sorrys to Great-Gran Beatrix's star in the sky.

'I could have phoned you,' I say, 'if I *had* a phone.'

'Come and eat,' says Mum.

I am suddenly starving, though my heart is still hammering from the horrors of what's just happened.

I sit down to roast chicken and roast potatoes, bread sauce and broccoli. It's my favourite, but I'm finding it hard to swallow.

Mum's smiling. Dad must be in a good mood.

I remember Old Alice's words: '*Don't ask, don't get.*'

'Dad,' I say, 'will you sponsor me?'

He laughs. 'When I saw the form wasn't on

the fridge I thought you'd given up on the idea.'

'No,' I say. 'I'm not giving up. Will you sponsor me?'

He laughs. 'All right then. Give me the form here.'

He writes:

Dad: £5.00 a length

'Wow, Dad! That's loads of money – thanks.' Through my sadness, a lovely warm feeling tingles up from my toes and bursts out through my smile.

'Right, I'm off to the Dog and Duck for a pint.' Dad snatches up the form. 'I'll take this with me. Get you some more sponsors.'

I give him a rare hug and a kiss on the cheek.

'Cheapest form I've ever filled in,' he continues, smirking. 'Bee, you should really stick to things you're good at, there's a good girl.' And he pats me on the head again.

My lips freeze in a big painted clown's smile. Dad doesn't believe in me. He doesn't believe in me one little bit.

I clonk up to my room and change into my bumblebee onesie. I play with the bees on my wall, lost in their world, my own world shattered.

I wake to the sound of what sounds like Dad trying to get his key in the lock. I am still fully clothed, with a felt bee scrunched up in my hand. I must have nodded off.

Dad might have got me more sponsors! I run to the stairs and sit halfway down, hugging my knees.

Mum comes out of the kitchen with her arms folded, lips pursed.

'Hello, my lovely family,' says Dad, staggering through the door. 'My lovely little Beatrix Daffodil.'

'Dad,' I say quickly, before digging deep for my best *I will be grateful for even one more sponsor* face. I swallow. 'Dad,' I ask, 'did you get me any sponsors?'

'Ta-dah,' says Dad, revealing my sponsor form with a flourish, like a magician with a silk handkerchief.

I snatch it. My form is full, completely full. My heart soars but then thuds to my toes.

Prince Harry. Usain Bolt. Beyoncé. Rita Ora. Harry Styles. Even Napoleon has sponsored me fifty pence a length, and he's been dead for ages.

On and on, I read more fake names – athletes, soap stars, politicians. I stare in horror.

'Dad, these aren't proper names. THESE ARE ALL FAMOUS PEOPLE.'

Mum leans through the banisters and takes the form from me.

'Oh, Mark, now we are going to have to pay all the money! Why didn't you check it?'

'Oh stop being grumpy, you pair of misery guts,' Dad says. 'I was just having a laugh. Bee can't swim, so no one will need to pay a penny anyway.'

Dad staggers into the kitchen and Mum stomps after him.

'Why can't you take anything seriously?' Mum screeches. 'Even your daughter's name is a joke to you. Beatrix Daffodil Tulip—'

I put my hands over my ears. My name's a joke. I'm a joke to my dad. Moon-Star's going and Bob and Old Alice are going . . . I run upstairs and slam my bedroom door.

I sit at my dressing table and look at my make-up.

I smear thick white base all over my face and paint the end of my nose red with a lipstick. With a black pencil, I draw pointy black stars round each eye, and then change back to the lipstick and add a huge sausage-shaped smile around my lips. I look in my mirror, my face surrounded by light bulbs.

'I'm just a clown,' I say out loud. 'A clumsy circus clown for people to laugh at.'

The make-up runs because of my tears. I wipe the tears away with my hands, but it smudges my careful work, which only makes me cry harder.

I can still hear arguing downstairs.

I reach out and touch my photos of Judy and Marilyn. They must have got sad from time to time. I wonder what they did to make themselves feel better when people didn't take them seriously? I wish I could talk to them. But most of all, I wish I could talk to Great-Gran Beatrix. I wonder if she has met Judy and Marilyn up in the sky. Maybe their stars are next to hers and she's told them all about me. Maybe she's told them that I'm a unique individual with dazzling style, or that I nearly drowned when I was three but I'm trying really hard not to be afraid of water.

Then all of a sudden, with every inch of my soul, I know that I must be brave and do the swim.

I wipe off my ruined clown make-up properly, using cleansing cream and tissues, and put on my red feather boa and bowler hat. I look in the mirror, hold my chin high and tell my reflection, 'My name is Beatrix Daffodil Tulip Chrysanthemum Rose Edwards, and I can do *anything*.'

23

'I can do anything,' I remind myself the next day, as I stand outside my classroom. Partridge is already droning on inside.

I take a deep breath and count to three to gather enough courage to knock on the door.

'One . . . one and a half. I can do anything . . .' I say. 'Well, *nearly* anything . . .'

I am soaked. Dad was already at work when I woke up, so I sneaked out a bucket from the garden shed and filled it from the hose pipe in the garden for Old Alice and Moon-Star. Doing twenty-five hops over a bridge with a heavy bucket of water was not a good idea.

When I got to the fence, I thought I could pour what water was left in my bucket through the fence and into Bob's bucket on the other side. So I shouted for Moon-Star, but he didn't come.

Old Alice came out to meet me instead. 'You've missed him, girl,' she said. 'Moon-Star and Bob have long gone to school.' Then she got Bob's bucket and I poured what water was left through the wire fence.

Old Alice looked me up and down, put her arm through the fence and adjusted my choice of hat for the day – a snuggly brown tweed deerstalker. She chuckled at me, but it wasn't in a mean way.

And now I'm wet and I've missed assembly and lessons have already started.

I pull up my stripy socks.

'Two . . . two and a half . . . Two and three quarters . . .'

Deep breath.

'Three.'

I knock.

'COME IN,' shouts Mrs Partridge.

I open the door and before I can even say anything she shouts, 'HAT, BEE!' and she swipes it off my head and puts it on her desk. 'It's so kind of you to join us at last,' she says, her eyes flashing.

Then she sees my socks.

'Bee, how many times?'

Then looks at my general sogginess.

'Have you been for a swim? Practising for tomorrow, are we?'

'You need it!' says Chrystal.

All the class laughs except Moon-Star.

I open my mouth to answer back.

'Just sit down, Bee,' Mrs Partridge snaps.

Moon-Star winks at me as I walk to our desk.

'Now, before you so rudely interrupted us, Bee, Chrystal was telling us about the dance gala.'

Chrystal tosses her hair, glares at me and starts off again, yakety-yakking about her freaky bendy tap-dancing antics.

Moon-Star isn't listening. He's drawing this amazing picture of Bob swimming under the moonlight with us splashing round him.

I pull my sponsor form out of my bag.

'Pssst! Moon-Star, look.' I put it on his lap.

'All those people,' I whisper, 'they're all fake names.'

And it's ripped from my hand as Mrs Partridge takes my form between her finger and thumb.

'And *what* is this?' she asks.

'It's my sponsor form, Mrs Partridge.'

'The corner looks like it has been chewed.'

'That was my horse what chewed it,' says Moon-Star, 'not Bee's fault, miss.'

'Quiet,' says Mrs Partridge, 'I'm talking to Bee. Well, at least you've managed to get some sponsors.' Then she looks at the names and her face quite literally turns purple.

'Is this meant to be a joke? The prime minister has sponsored you, has he, Bee?'

'No, Mrs Partridge, it was my dad's friends having a laugh – but they'll pay.'

'This is a disgrace! I have a good mind not to let you do the swim.'

Moon-Star stands up so fast his chair clatters down behind him. 'Bee has more right to do that swim than any of you, do you hear? Her Great-

Gran Beatrix passed away, who she loved and is called after, and she lived in the Rise and Shine Happy Care Home for Old People so 'tis right that Bee does the swim! For her gran's memory.'

Tiny tears spark at the back of my eyes as a whisper of a breath catches in my throat and I sit really, really still. This is another all-time best moment of my life.

'MOON-STAR HIGGINS, SIT DOWN. THE DAY YOU CAN WRITE A LETTER EXPRESSING YOUR OPINION IS THE DAY I WILL LISTEN!' shouts Mrs Partridge.

There is a shocked silence.

My brain boils.

Slowly, slowly I reach out my hand to Moon-Star and link my thumb to his.

Mrs Partridge looks flustered; I think she knows she's gone too far. It serves her right if she can't sleep at night. If she can't sleep ever again.

Then Moon-Star walks to the whiteboard and writes:

BEE WILL SWIM.

24

Only one more sleep to go. Tomorrow, I will be attempting to swim two lengths in front of all those people. I feel the terrors from top to toe.

Moon-Star's words ring in my ears. He told me, '*Your legs is stronger now, Bee. You'll do them two lengths they say you gotta do, easy. Me and Bob just knows it.*'

But me, I'm not so sure. I'm sitting on my bed looking down at my legs and they just feel wobbly. Splashing about in the reflection of the moonbeams in our secret pool, with Moon-Star and Bob beside me, is one thing, but swimming in the sponsored swim in front of all those people . . . well, that's quite another.

It's Friday night, so Dad is working late at the office. Mum and I are having fish and chips for tea. The radio is on and Mum is singing along. I feel hungry, and I'm trying to eat, but all I can think about is THE SPONSORED SWIM.

'Eat up, Bee,' says Mum, 'the chips are nice and crispy, just how you like them.'

So I smile and dip my chips in ketchup and try to eat and sing along with Mum at the same time.

There's a knock at the door. Mum goes to answer it.

I can hear mumbling. It's Moon-Star! I run into the hall.

He's standing there, talking to my mum. '. . . Bee's forgotten, I think, Mrs Edwards. But we got to go and visit that Rise and Shine Home for Old People. It's cos of the sponsored swim thing. Mrs Partridge said me and Bee got to do it. Look – I'm bringing them some honey.'

He holds out a large jar.

'But,' I begin to say.

Moon-Star glares at me. 'Come on, Bee. Quick, we don't want to let the old people down.'

And he walks into the hall, grabs my wrist and pulls me out.

'But what about—' says Mum.

But we've gone before she can finish.

'Moon-Star Higgins, what a pack of lies,' I say, 'big fat juicy ones. Mrs Partridge did not tell us to visit the Rise and Shine Home.'

Moon-Star winks. 'No, but *I* say we're going to visit. Come on, Bee, get a wiggle on.'

I dig my heels into the ground. 'I can't go in there, I just can't.'

'Bee, these old folks are your friends. Linford and Millie are waiting.'

'Moon-Star, you don't understand.'

'I do,' says Moon-Star. 'I understand perfectly that you will never be happy until you accept that your Great-Gran Beatrix has gone and she's now just memories. And you got to hug those memories and hold 'em tight, but you also gotta live your life, Bee.'

'But I'm never going to see her again,' I say, and I feel a big fat tear splashing down my cheek.

'Not on this planet, no,' Moon-Star says. 'But she's with you, Bee, and I know she's proud of you learning to swim when you're so afraid. She's with you in here.' He taps his heart with his screwed-up fist. 'If I can sit in a classroom, you can have tea with the old folks. Now come on, Bee, find your courage.'

Next thing I know, I'm following him down the path.

'I'll go in there on one condition,' I tell him. 'You come and watch me swim tomorrow. You will, won't you? You won't leave before . . .'

'I'll be there.'

Moon-Star rings the doorbell.

'Promise?' I ask.

Moon-Star spits on his hand and I spit on mine and we shake hands.

Linford opens the door, bows and holds his arm out.

'Miss Bee, how lovely to see you. If you would like to come this way.'

So I take Linford's arm and Moon-Star walks behind us. There is no escape now.

He takes me into the room they call their parlour. Matilda is at the piano, playing a mixture of tunes from old Marilyn films – 'Diamonds Are a Girl's Best Friend' and 'We Are Two Girls From Little Rock' – and there is Great-Gran Beatrix's old and ragged brown armchair, sagging in the middle. It's empty. I can see her sitting there as if it were yesterday and the memories choke me, so I turn away.

In the middle of the room there is a table laid with a beautiful ruby-red cloth and Great-Gran Beatrix's cups and saucers and cutlery. Mabel is counting the places and Sid is shining the glasses with a cloth.

Millie is sitting at the table. She gets up and gives me a kiss.

'Sit down, Bee,' she twinkles.

Linford pulls a chair out for me. There are four places set. Moon-Star sits down in the chair next to mine.

But there is something else. By each plate is a mug with painted pictures of Dorothy and the Tin Man and the Lion and Toto, and they are all looking up at a shiny star.

'Did you . . . ?' I ask Moon-Star.

'Yip,' he says, 'I painted 'em special so you can remember her.'

No words come.

Everyone starts to chatter but I just hold my Dorothy mug in my hand and smile.

After tea, they lead me to Great-Gran

Beatrix's chair.

'Sit down,' says Linford.

I take a deep breath and lower myself into her armchair. As soon as I do, it hugs me in memories.

Millie wraps me in the rainbow blanket.

'I'm so sorry that I've never been to tea before, I . . .' Then the words run out.

'We know,' says Linford.

And we watch *The Wizard of Oz*, just like I used to do with Great-Gran Beatrix.

It's really late outside but I hear Linford phone Mum and talk in hushed whispers. We watch till we are all sleepy.

I look round at all the old people who have wrapped me in kindness, and I know from the bottom of my heart that I've got to do my very best in the swim tomorrow.

When the film is finished, Moon-Star walks me back across the road, our thumbs linked.

Mum is at the open door, waiting.

'Go to your ma,' says Moon-Star. 'Sleep well, Bee.' And he disappears into the shadows.

I run into Mum's arms.

'She's gone, Mum. Great-Gran Beatrix . . . she's gone and she's never coming back.'

'I know, Bee,' Mum whispers into my hair. 'I know, my darling; she was my gran too and I miss her. Oh I miss her so, so much, it aches.'

And Mum hugs me tight until I can't breathe, our tears mingling into one river.

I scramble upstairs to my bedroom and fling open my drawer, hands searching. I pull out the final hat that Great-Gran Beatrix gave me – the rubber swimming cap with the bees all over it – and put it on the final peg on my hatstand. Then I open my bee notebook and write:

Goodbye, Great-Gran Beatrix.

I lean out of my window, hold the book open at that page and imagine the words peeling off the page and swimming to the moon, so Great-Gran Beatrix can read them from her star.

'Goodbye,' I shout into the night sky.

25

The first thing I hear as I wake is rain splattering against the window. The first thing I see, through my half-closed eyelashes, is the swimming hat, hanging on the hatstand. I bolt upright.

IT'S TODAY! THE SPONSORED SWIM IS TODAY!

Even though I'm shivering with fear, my heart feels warm at the thought of Moon-Star watching me swim later.

Somehow – somehow – I get through the day, but the seconds are like minutes, the minutes like hours and the hours like days.

For the millionth time I wish I had a phone, then I could text Moon-Star, but then I remember that he's not got a phone either so it wouldn't be much use.

I go upstairs to pack my swimming bag, chucking in my towel and a hairbrush. I check I've got my inhaler, then I carefully tuck my bee notebook and a pen underneath my towel. Finally, I reach for the swimming cap, my hands shaking, and gently place it inside my bag.

I wriggle into my swimming costume, then put on my clothes over the top, tucking my jeans into my DMs. I top it all off with my bowler hat.

Looking in my dressing-table mirror, I tilt the brim back with jaunty style, and picture Great-Gran Beatrix standing behind me in the mirror, smiling. I smile back.

'*You have dazzling style, my darling; hold your head up high and show the world how you sparkle,*' she says, then the memory mist clears and she's gone.

So I add my Marilyn dress to the bag. No reason why I shouldn't look nice when they make me give out programmes and move chairs and everything else they're going to make me do to help at the dance extravaganza. Why should Chrystal have all the good costumes?

'Time to go,' shouts Dad up the stairs. 'I want to get there early – parking will be murder.'

My tummy does a flip-flop and I walk, jelly-legged, down the stairs.

'Hurry!' calls Mum, and she locks the door and we run to the car. It's now pouring with rain.

I climb into the back seat and fasten my seat belt as the windscreen wipers drive the sheets of rain off the window.

Dad starts the car. 'Good things on telly tonight,' he says. 'Shouldn't take too long, this sponsor thing, should it, Bee? We'll be home in no time.'

'Mark,' says Mum, 'I told you. I've booked us tickets for the dance gala afterwards, too.'

'What dance gala? I don't know about a dance gala.'

Mum turns round from the front seat and rolls her eyes at me.

Dad laughs. 'You're not dancing too, are

you, Bee? Two left feet, like your mother. Good thing you don't do ballet any more – that was a waste of money!'

Mum's eyes widen. 'Mark!'

'No, Dad,' I say, screwing my hands into such tight fists, my nails cut into the palms. 'They'll have me moving chairs and things. It'll be the Chrystal Kelly show. You'll have to watch her doing tap, ballet, jazz, gymnastics, hip-hop, and it will go on for ever and—'

'Oh, will Mayor Kelly be there?' Dad interrupts. 'Good, sounds like a great evening. Bet he's proud of Chrystal – such a talented girl.'

I give him my very best *you haven't hurt my feelings at all, Dad* face but he doesn't see, as he is concentrating on driving up the rainy road, past the Russian-doll houses.

The rain seems to be getting heavier and heavier. The car splashes through puddles. We pass Chrystal's house. Bryony is outside, holding an umbrella over Chrystal. Mayor Kelly steps out of his front door. Dad parps his horn and waves. I duck down in shame, bumping my head on the window.

As we go over the bridge I close my eyes and count. But my eyes snap straight open once we reach the other side. I peer through the trees, past the hateful fence, and relief floods through me as I spot a flash of the red wagon. Old Alice and Moon-Star are still there. I knew Moon-Star would keep his promise. I can see Bob's hooves waving in the air as he rolls on the ground, but there's no sign of Moon-Star. He must have left for the swimming pool.

Mum turns round and smiles. 'Looking forward to the swim, Bee?'

I nod a lie.

The windows are steaming up as we drive through Ashton and search for a space in the car park. There are umbrellas and children and old people everywhere.

Imogen waves at me as we walk into the leisure centre. 'Come on, Bee. There are two swimmers to a lane. It's written on the whiteboard over here. I'll show you.'

And then I see it:

LANE 2: Chrystal Kelly and Beatrix Edwards

Oh no!

'Will you swap with me, Imogen, please, please, pleeeease?' I beg.

'Sorry, Bee, I'm in Lily's lane.' Imogen shrugs. 'Good luck.' She disappears into the changing room.

I feel like crying but I'm not going to. Instead, I find an empty cubicle, strip down to my swimming costume and pull on the bee swimming cap for the first time ever. It fits my head perfectly. Then I reach into my bag for the bee notebook and flick through it. It opens at:

> *Aerodynamically, the bee shouldn't be able to fly,*
> *but the bee doesn't know it so goes on flying anyway.*
> **Mary Kay Ash**

'Thank you, Great-Gran Beatrix,' I whisper. It's perfect – the bee isn't built to be able to fly but it does it anyway. Everyone thinks I shouldn't be able to do the sponsored swim, but I'll do it anyway. I'll show them.

I write in my notebook:

I, BEE, WILL SWIM TWO LENGTHS.

Then I tuck the book away and walk out of the changing room, splashing through the shower and on to the swimming pool. My towel and inhaler go on a bench at the side.

I look up at the gallery for Moon-Star, but he's not there. Panic ripples through my body. Instead, the gallery is full of old people from the Rise and Shine Happy Care Home for Older People. Sid, Matilda and Mabel all smile and nudge each other when they see me.

Mum and Dad are in the front row. They wave. Dad shouts out, 'Bee, don't fall into the swimming pool before you even begin, will you!' then laughs so loudly at his own unfunny joke that other people turn round.

OH THE SHAME. I pretend I haven't heard.

Mayor Kelly is also in the front row, all puffed up and pleased with himself. Mrs Kelly and Mitzi are next to him, wearing matching white tracksuits. Mrs Partridge is there too, sat beside a little bald man, who must be her husband. He looks a bit scared.

But I still can't see Moon-Star. Where is he? I can't do this without him. He promised . . . But what if he had no choice? What if, while I was changing, Moon-Star and Old Alice were being evicted? It's a day early, but I wouldn't put anything past Mayor Kelly.

Bryony is giving Chrystal a pep talk at the start of our lane. I walk up and down the side of the pool, shivering, searching the gallery for Moon-Star, my ears echoing with the chattering voices.

A lifeguard blows his whistle. Mr Gregory is standing beside him, with Linford and Millie, who are wearing orange T-shirts with 'We Love Bungee Jumping' written on the front.

As I walk past Linford he whispers, 'Make your great-gran proud,' then he turns to all the waiting swimmers. 'Now remember, do your best,' he says to them, 'that's all we ask of you. Swimming your two lengths for us today will make such a difference to our lives. Of course, if you want to do more, that would also be lovely!'

I walk to the start of my lane, where the water stretches out in front of me. The far end looks such a long way off I might as well be swimming to the moon and back. My eyes sweep the gallery one last time. Still no sign of Moon-Star. I can't do this without him, I just can't . . . But then I hear Great-Gran Beatrix's voice saying, 'Promise me you'll learn to swim', so I shut my eyes and shuffle to the edge of the pool until my toes are over the edge.

Another whistle blows. I hold my nose and jump. I come up spluttering, facing the wrong way round, the chlorine stinging my eyes.

'Ew, you splashed me!' squeals Chrystal, then she pulls her goggles over her eyes, dives above my head and is off in front of me, speeding through the water.

I push off from the side and do a doggy

paddle. One, two – one, two – one, two. My head is above water, my legs are kicking, I'm moving in the right direction.

One, two – one, two – one, two.

'GO ON, BEE!' I hear Mum shout from the gallery.

One, two – one, two – one, two.

I see Chrystal ahead of me as she reaches the end of her first length, does a somersault underwater and starts her second length in front crawl. She is ploughing back towards me, getting nearer and nearer. I keep going. The water from her arms splashes me as she passes.

Something grabs my ankle. I'm being pulled down. The waters are getting me. Chrystal's wide open eyes lock with mine underwater – hers big with spite, mine with fear. I kick out with my other leg, getting her in the ribs, and she lets go. We both come up spluttering.

'You swim like a dog, Bee,' she hisses at me.

'Bendy tap-dancing freak,' I hiss back and she's off again, kicking water in my eyes as she tornadoes away.

I tread water and look around. Surely someone saw that? Chrystal nearly drowned me! But Mum and Dad are arguing, Mayor Kelly is talking to Imogen's mum, Mrs Kelly is giving Mitzi lots of little kisses, Bryony is taking a sneaky peek at a magazine on her lap.

I start to doggy paddle forward. Ahead of me in another lane, Timothy Lee has reached the end of his first length, coughing and spluttering. Everyone cheers as the lifeguard helps him out of the water and up the swimming pool steps.

I smile. At least the second most useless person at sports managed a length.

'WELL DONE, TIMOTHY!' I shout.

If he can do it then I can.

One, two – one, two – one, two.

My legs feel heavy, and my arms are starting to ache.

One, two – one, two – one, two. I'm nearly . . . nearly . . . nearly there. One, two – one, two.

And I reach out until my hand clasps the side of the pool.

I'VE DONE IT! I'VE SWUM A LENGTH!

Mum waves and cheers.

Dad's mouth is open in shock.

Mrs Partridge looks a bit surprised.

I search and search for Moon-Star in the gallery but he's still not there. My heart sinks; he must have been evicted. I'll never see him again.

I hear Great-Gran Beatrix's voice in my head. 'Swim for me, munchkin, swim for me.'

So I turn around and push off from the side, my tired legs kicking.

One, two – one, two – doggy-paddle – one, two – one, two.

I remember to breathe and slowly . . . slowly, I move forward through the water.

Ahead of me, Chrystal has already reached the end of her second length. Mrs Kelly is standing by the poolside, holding out the biggest towel you ever saw in your life.

One, two – one, two – one, two – my legs and arms get heavier and heavier.

'Come on, Bee, you can do it,' I say out loud.

Chrystal pats herself down with the towel and starts doing backflips along the side of the pool. The lifeguard blows a whistle at her to stop but she carries on.

I'm so close now . . . one, two – one, two – one, two.

AND I'M THERE. TWO LENGTHS!

Everyone is ignoring Chrystal and clapping me.

'SO PROUD OF YOU, BEE,' shouts Mum.

Dad looks very shocked.

Mrs Partridge looks very, very surprised.

But the one person I want to clap me is not there. Moon-Star, where are you?

Chrystal, who has now stopped flipping, stamps her foot. With her face purple and her mouth turned down at the corners, she starts to screech.

'WHAT ARE YOU EVEN DOING HERE? YOU CAN'T EVEN SWIM!'

There is a deathly hush.

'Oh but I can, Chrystal, I can,' I say.

'Well done, Bee! I'll meet you in the foyer,'

shouts Dad from the gallery.

I look from Dad to Chrystal and from Chrystal to Dad.

Then I give them both a cheeky little wave AND I PUSH OFF FOR MY THIRD LENGTH.

As I go, I do my best *you should have believed in me* face. I don't care if Dad sees it or not, but Judy and Marilyn would be proud.

I try a calm, gentle breaststroke this time, breathing deeply as I go – one and two – one and two.

One and two. I am in my own world.

The voices in the gallery and the splashing of other swimmers tinkle in my brain, as if they are far, far away.

Up ahead, I see something white oozing from the window. I blink hard, so that the white blob will fall out of my eyes. I need to concentrate on my swimming. But there it is again.

One, two – one, two.

It's getting bigger.

It's a big white puffy leg hanging through the window!

I blink again, and another leg appears, followed by a body and a gigantic white head. For a minute I think it's an astronaut. Then I realise it's someone in a beekeeping suit. My heart thuds.

The white puffy figure jumps down from the window ledge and sprints to the ladders that reach up to the diving boards. Up he goes to the first ladder, then the second, then the very top board. The lifeguard starts climbing the ladder after him.

The figure reveals his face – it's Moon-Star! He lets down a banner made from a bed sheet. It says:

QUEEN BEE

And suddenly, I don't feel the cold of the swimming pool water. I know that without a doubt, whether he's with me or not, our souls are joined for ever and ever. This is a moment I shall never forget for as long as I am on planet earth.

Everyone is cheering as the lifeguard escorts Moon-Star back down the ladders. I reach the end of my third length and push away, floating on my back so I can watch Moon-Star as they take him away. He turns and smiles, gives me a little wave and then is gone.

I flip over on to my front. The pain in my legs and arms has gone and I keep on moving forward, cos I'm Queen Bee.

I reach the end of my fourth length.

'GET OUT OF THE POOL!' Dad shouts. 'BEE, GET OUT OF THE POOL, RIGHT NOW!'

He looks panicked and then it hits me that he will have to pay all the money of the people who sponsored me in the pub.

EVERY SINGLE PENNY.

I give Dad a naughty little wave and carry on swimming. I can hear Mum laughing. Up and down I swim. Up and down. I try front crawl, then back crawl. I even try butterfly but quickly go back to doggy-paddle. They may not really be proper strokes but they are Queen Bee's proper strokes.

I see the other kids gradually getting out of the pool, till there is only me left and I'm still on fire.

I swim my eighth length. My legs feel like lead and my arms like they have weights strapped to them. One and twooooo. Every bit of me aches. One AND TWOOOOOOOOOOOOO.

'PLEASE, BEE. PLEASE GET OUT. GET OUT!' shouts Dad.

I ignore him and carry on.

One and twooooooooooooooooooo.

Everyone is cheering me as I reach the end of my tenth length.

The lifeguard pulls me out of the water. My jelly legs cannot hold me up and I sink to the ground.

Linford and Millie are crying.

'You did it, munchkin, you did it,' cheers Millie.

'Your great-gran would have been so proud,' says Linford.

Mum and Dad have come down to the poolside. Mum grabs my towel and inhaler from the bench. A little baby elephant is climbing on to my chest. I breathe out and Mum pushes my inhaler gently into my mouth. I breathe in as the dose hits me and hold for ten.

'Well, Mark,' says Mum to Dad, 'I've worked out that you owe Bee fifty pounds, plus the five hundred and sixty pounds that you will have to pay for all the silly people from the pub who sponsored her under false names. Oh, and by the way, you also owe her a phone.'

Dad is as white as a ghost. He tries to smile at me but his lips wobble.

Mum wraps me in a towel and gives me the biggest hug. I think we both know that things will never be the same again.

'Well done, Queen Bee,' she says and gives me a wink.

'Bee,' I hear Dad's voice calling.

I turn around.

'I'm proud of you,' he says, smiling.

And I know he means it.

26

Mum walks me to the changing room, her arm round my shoulder.

'I did it, Mum! I finally kept my promise – I learned to swim. I just wish Great-Gran Beatrix had been here to see it. I wish she knew.'

'I believe she does,' says Mum, squeezing my shoulder. 'And your friend Moon-Star made quite an entrance . . .'

'Mum, I need to get changed quick,' I suddenly realise. 'I need to find him!'

But with my jelly legs, it's hard changing in a hurry. I keep getting my clothes back to front and inside out, so Mum has to help me, as if I am a baby again.

I pull the Marilyn dress from my bag and

shake out the creases. I kick my vest into my bag.

'I'm wearing this,' I say.

'Where did you get that from?' asks Mum.

'Old Alice made it for me,' I reply.

'You look lovely,' says Mum, doing up the back and turning me round.

'Quick, Mum, please – we need to hurry! I want to see Moon-Star before he goes off with his mum and Old Alice.'

I don't have any dainty pointy high heels like Marilyn, so I shove on my DMs. Mum brushes my hair as I stuff my wet swimming things into my bag – all apart from the bumblebee swimming hat, which I fold with love and tuck into a corner. I can hear wind outside, so I put my bowler hat into the top of my bag and do up the zip. I can't lose the bowler to the wind's rage.

I grab Mum's hand and pull her into the swimming pool foyer, but Moon-Star is nowhere to be seen.

Dad is pacing up and down impatiently.

When he sees us he taps his watch.

'Come on,' he says. 'I want to get good seats – Mayor Kelly and his men have already gone through. It would be good to sit near them. I might get to talk to him in the interval.'

I am too tired to dig deep and give him my *you make me sick* face. I bet even Marilyn and Judy couldn't do acting after swimming ten lengths in a sponsored swim. We are getting pushed forward by the throngs of people trying to get next door to the town hall dance extravaganza.

There's a thunderclap. As I step outside Mum holds her coat over my head.

'Come on,' she says and as we run, my dress gets tiny splatters of mud on it.

They have put boards over the puddles at the entrance of the town hall. Mrs Partridge is at the door. I think she is trying to smile at me but it seems to be a bit hard for her face.

I've got to find Moon-Star before he goes, but I'm trapped by Mrs Partridge. 'Ah, Beatrix Daffodil – didn't you surprise us all . . .' The next bit comes out very quickly: 'Yesverywelldone swimmingtoday.' Then the next bit is loud and clear: 'Now, make yourself useful!' and she dumps the biggest pile of programmes into my aching arms. 'Give these out.'

As Mum and Dad disappear to find seats, all my ten-length glory vanishes; no one is cheering me now. People just snatch programmes from my hands and I drop the whole pile of them twice.

Mrs Partridge tuts and waves her hands impatiently towards the audience for me to hand them out quicker.

I see the old people from the Rise and Shine Happy Care Home for Older People sitting in the reserved seats in the front two rows and I walk down the aisle to give them each a programme. When they see me, they all cheer, 'Well done, Bee!'

Matilda is humming a tune to herself and tapping the beats out on her knee. Sid is adjusting a cushion beneath his bottom so that he can see the stage over the head of the tall person in front of him. Mabel looks as if she's nodding off, but her head snaps up as I pass her and she does a loud bingo call: 'Jump and jive, twenty-five!'

Linford has his arm round Millie and waves his programme in the air to show he's already got one. I wave back, dropping all the programmes again, but as I bend to pick them up a flash of scarlet catches my eye from the stage. It's Chrystal, standing in the wings. Madame Bertha is behind her, scraping her curls back into a bun and spraying Chrystal's hair with hairspray. Chrystal is in a scarlet costume covered in sequins.

Mrs Kelly is fussing round her, clutching Mitzi. She calls out, 'Remember, darling, smile and point your toes,' then she disappears from view.

A group of girls also in red sequinned dresses – though with fewer sequins than Chrystal's dress – huddle around her as she whispers and points to me.

She sees me watching and smirks. I give her my very best *you don't bother me, I've just swum ten lengths* face and turn my back, pushing my way through the crowds, still searching, searching for Moon-Star. Mayor Kelly walks on to the stage; people nudge each other and the chatter subsides.

'Before the dance extravaganza starts, the volunteers have been totalling up the sponsor forms. Everyone has done very well but special mention must go to Beatrix Edwards, who has raised an enormous six hundred and seventy pounds.'

Everyone cheers. Dad looks sick. I blush with pride. I feel Great-Gran Beatrix's arms hugging me and I miss her, I miss her, I miss her.

Then Mayor Kelly drones on a bit but I'm not listening. I just want to find Moon-Star before he moves on. When the mayor finishes, everyone claps – and my dad cheers. More shame!

Suddenly, the music strikes up and the dance extravaganza begins.

Ballet and tap and hip-hop and gymnastics and more ballet and tap – all of it starring

Chrystal in various spangly costumes. On and on and on it goes.

Until the music stops and Chrystal walks to the front of the stage.

'Ladies and gentleman,' she says, 'boys and girls, and our honoured guests from the Rise and Shine Happy Care Home for Older People. For our last number, we have a surprise. At school, we sometimes do what we call a dance-off. We stand in a circle and take it in turns to go in the middle and show dance moves we've made up. We'd like to do a dance-off on stage today.'

Madame Bertha stands up from her seat in the front row. This is obviously not part of the show. She shakes her cane at Chrystal, who ignores her and carries on.

'We've all voted that Bee Edwards should get to go first in the dance-off, as she raised the most money in the swim.'

I go icy cold as Chrystal's words hit the air. My jelly legs are back. I shake my head.

'No,' I whisper. The next comes out as a

shout, 'NO!'

People turn round and stare.

Chrystal starts clapping and chanting, 'Bee, Bee, Bee,' and everyone copies her.

'Bee, Bee, Bee,' they all chorus and I have no choice but to walk up to the stage with my jelly legs wobbling.

I try to hold my head high and pretend I'm Marilyn and do a wiggle-waggle walk, but all I can hear are my boots clomping. I climb up on to the stage and Chrystal starts clicking her fingers to start up a rhythm – *click-click stomp*, *click-click stomp*. The others make a circle around me and join in. *Click-click stomp*, *click-click stomp*. But my body won't move and the clicking and stomping gradually stops and there is a forever silence as I feel hundreds of pairs of eyes on me.

'Go on, Bee,' shouts Linford, but I just stand there. I can't dance. I can't. I'm the most rubbish dancer ever. I can't even walk without tripping up. And then I remember a special dance. The first dance ever on this planet, the one that was danced more than a hundred and fifty million years ago. THE ANCIENT WAGGLE DANCE OF THE BEES.

So I waggle my hips. A few people laugh but the clapping starts up again, so I do it again. Another laugh. Then I dance the bee waggle dance for my life. First I stick my uncurtseying type of bottom out as far as it will go and waggle up to Chrystal and pretend I am giving her nectar.

She smirks and whispers, 'Got you now, haven't I, Bee? You can't dance and everyone can see it.'

But I am a worker honeybee so I ignore her and wiggle up to Susan and Ruth and other girls from Madame Bertha's in the circle. I imagine that the nectar I have gathered is sweeter than all the other bees' nectar and I pretend that all the clapping girls in the circle are other bees admiring me. I start to waggle in a straight line to show them they have to fly straight ahead to find the flowers. As it's such fine nectar, I wiggle my bee behind even faster – then I loop in a circle to the right, wiggle in a straight line and loop to the left.

My waggle dance is the finest waggle dance of all. But people are laughing and laughing and laughing. My face is on fire and I want to die.

Mum has stood up and she's holding out her arms to me, looking really upset.

Then from the back of the hall comes a strange, haunting melody. I stop and look to see Old Alice walking up the aisle, playing her harmonica. Behind her is Daisy with bells round her ankles and following her is Moon-Star with bare feet, rolled-up jeans and a torn white shirt, carrying one of the puddle boards from outside. They walk up the steps and on to the stage. The audience is silent.

Daisy takes my hands. 'Come on child, dance with me.' She nods at me to take my boots off. I throw them in the corner and Daisy starts her bewitching, mesmerising dance, twirling and whirling around faster and faster and faster and then she beckons me and twirls me around and makes me shine like she does, and my legs and arms don't feel awkward. I have rhythm, I have style, and everyone is clapping.

As I pass Chrystal she stamps her foot and hisses, 'This is my show.'

So I stick out my tongue at her and carry on dancing to the strange melody that tells of lands far away.

Then Moon-Star squashes his feet into my clumpy, clumpy DM boots and starts to do the Gypsy step dance on the board and the audience claps as his feet get faster and faster and wilder and wilder until even Madame Bertha is smiling and clapping.

Then the music stops. Old Alice walks to the front of the stage.

There's a hushed silence.

'Good people of Ashton,' she says. 'This is our farewell to you. I am just an old woman, living in peace with my young grandson, and you have taken away our water. You put up a fence and you caged us in like animals. Then you ordered us off our land. Well, you've won.

But we will leave with the dignity that you tried to take away from us. This music and this dance is our parting gift to you.'

Moon-Star hands me back my boots. I shove them back on my feet.

'Please,' I say, 'please, Moon-Star, we can fight this.'

Moon-Star won't look me in the eye, but he links his thumb in mine for a second.

And with that, Old Alice, Daisy and Moon-Star walk down the steps of the stage and along the aisle, out of the hall.

'Stop! Please don't let them go!' I call to everyone. 'What about the bees? There must always be a traveller living in the clearing, or the bees will swarm! It says so on the Promise Tree. Without the bees we will have no flowers and vegetables. And Old Alice, she feeds the cats. We will be overrun with mice and rats . . .'

But no one is listening. They are getting up from their seats and pushing towards the door.

I jump up and down, trying to get even a glimpse of Moon-Star, but he has gone.

27

'MOON-STAR!' I shout. 'MOON-STAAAAAAR!'

'Bee, over here,' Mum calls, from her seat. She and Dad are putting on their coats.

'Bee, come over here. NOW!' shouts Dad.

I ignore them, clawing my way through the crowds that are blocking the door. People are tutting at me.

But when I get outside, Moon-Star, Old Alice and Daisy are nowhere to be seen.

I protect my eyes from the sheets of rain as I look up and down the road, searching for Moon-Star's white shirt among all the dark overcoats and umbrellas.

Dad grabs my wrist. 'I can't believe you showed us up like that. I told you not to talk to those people! GET TO THE CAR.' And he starts dragging me towards it.

'No, Mark,' says Mum, through the rain. 'Bee's standing up for what she believes in. You should be proud of her.'

I stamp hard on Dad's foot in my clumpy DM boots and he lets go.

I've got to get to Moon-Star before he goes for ever.

Dad races after me, yelling my name.

I run through the town square, towards the road leading out of the village, and double back on myself, through the tunnel of wire, fighting against the wet branches as they hit me in the face.

I hide behind a tree and listen . . . No footsteps or calling. Must have given Dad the slip. I look up and see the branches of the Promise Tree soaring high in the sky. I run to it, reaching out to touch its bark. A dark cloud casts a shadow on the full moon. The bees in the hives are silent.

Gulping in mouthfuls of rain-drenched air to

banish the lurking elephant, I stagger up the path, then stop still.

No red wagon.

No Daisymobile.

No Bob.

I'm too late. They've really gone this time.

I see something white under some stones. I kick them out of the way. It's a wet piece of paper. As I pick it up, gold coins tumble out of it, revealing smudged words:

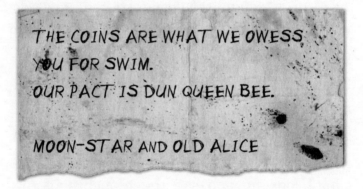

THE COINS ARE WHAT WE OWESS
YOU FOR SWIM.
OUR PACT IS DUN QUEEN BEE.

MOON-STAR AND OLD ALICE

My heart shatters into a thousand pieces.

The rain stops and is replaced by an eerie silence. Then a flash of lightning.

A rat runs over my foot. I shudder. Cats! Where are the cats? My eyes search the nooks and crannies of the woods, but they are nowhere to be seen.

Then a strange humming fills the air. It gets louder and louder and louder and a cloud rises from the hives.

The bees are swarming. The prophecy has come true.

A scream cuts through the humming, ricocheting off the tree and heading to the moon. Then I realise my mouth is open wide and the scream is coming from me . . . from my soul.

28

'Bee? Bee, where are you?'

Another flash of lightning reveals Dad and Mum, stumbling through the clearing. Mum is carrying my bag.

'MOON-STAR'S GONE,' I cry out.

'Bee, darling,' says Mum, rummaging through my bag, 'you're wheezing.'

I hadn't even noticed the elephant stamping on my chest. Mum hands me the inhaler but I knock her hand away.

'Take it. Now,' she says.

So I do, and as I hold my breath and count 1, 2, 3, 4, 5, 6, 7, I wish with all my heart that a miracle will happen and by the time I get to ten Moon-Star will appear.

8, 9, 10.

But he doesn't.

Dad lifts me over his shoulder in a fireman's lift.

'Put me down! I have to find Moon-Star!'

I kick my legs against his back, but he totally ignores me and yells over his shoulder to Mum, 'If that wire fence wasn't there we could have walked home. As it is, we're better going back for the car.'

I struggle more but it's no use – we make our way back through the trees and to the town square, where our battered blue car stands alone.

Dad puts me in the back seat, slams the door, gets in the front with Mum and starts the car.

I open my door, preparing to jump out. Mum screams. Dad screeches to a halt. I leap out of the car, but Dad's too quick. He jumps out, grabs me, puts me back in the car, clonks my seat belt on and jumps in the front again. Next thing I hear is the click of the child lock.

We drive in silence. I HATE HIM, I HATE HIM, I HATE HIM.

It starts to rain again, great sheets of it. A wind buffets the car, and the trees sway dangerously. The river is already rising as we drive on to the crooked bridge.

I begin to count, but I've only got to nineteen when there's a loud creak. My breath stops, Mum screams, Dad puts down the accelerator and the car screeches forward.

I count for my life and reach twenty-five just as we cross on to the other side, but there's a sudden squealing of wood and nails behind us. I turn to look out of the back window and watch in horror as the bridge comes crashing down, followed by a tree that slides down the mudbank and topples across the river, leaving its roots clawing at the sky.

My thoughts freeze. Dad stops the car. I'm aware that Mum is quietly sobbing.

Dad puts one hand on her knee, and his other hand shakes on the steering wheel.

The waters won! They got the bridge and that tree, and they nearly got us . . . I can't feel my legs and arms, my teeth are chattering and

I'm suddenly three again, dancing for Great-Gran Beatrix, spinning and spinning, then SPLASH! – into the waters, getting sucked down further and further . . .

'Are you OK, Bee?' Dad asks.

I grit my chattering teeth and nod a lie. He turns round and reaches for my hand, Mum twists round and grabs my other hand, and we sit there not speaking, the wind lashing the car. Eventually, Dad starts the engine and the car judders forward again.

We reach the Russian-doll houses. Dad slams on the brakes as Chrystal runs out into the road, in front of the car. We all scramble out.

Chrystal's mouth is open wide and twisted, her face distorted.

'Help! PLEASE HELP! It's my little brother . . .'

'Daniel!' I tear down the wet path, the rain cutting my face.

Chrystal's front door is open and a scream rips the air in two. 'MY BABY, MY BABY, MY BABY.'

Mitzi is howling, somewhere in the house.

My heart turns cold. I race up the stairs and into Daniel's nursery. Chrystal's mum is holding Daniel, crying. The little boy's eyes are rolling and his breath's rattling.

Mayor Kelly is pacing up and down, shouting, 'Where's the ambulance? Why isn't it here?'

'The bridge is down, Mr Kelly,' Dad tells him, from behind me. 'The ambulance won't be able to reach Little Ash.'

I watch as Mayor Kelly stops still and goes pale, then it comes to me in a flash.

'Old Alice!' I say. 'You need Old Alice – she's a healer. She stopped me wheezing. I'm going to find her – they can't have gone that far in this weather!' And before they can stop me I'm down the stairs, out of the door, slip-sliding down the path and fighting through the sheets of rain.

I hear Mum and Dad yelling at me to come back, to stop, but I ignore them. Then I hear a tree crashing down behind me, but I still don't look back.

Running, skidding, tripping over broken branches in the road, I make my way to the river, but when I reach it, my heart hits the floor. The black waters rear up, sending icy cold fingers towards me, calling me into their depths, roaring in my head.

I peer through the dark. I can't be sure, but the tree that crashed over the river is so tall it looks like it might have reached the opposite bank. Even if it hasn't, it's the only way to get near the other side, so I kick off my heavy mud-splattered DMs and grab hold of the tree's roots, pulling myself along. The muddy bank squelches between my toes as I haul myself up on to the trunk then carefully ease myself on to my hands and knees. I start to crawl, slowly, slowly, trying to keep my limbs under control . . . one and two and three and four . . . I keep counting as I go, crawling my way forward, bit by bit. I'm getting closer to the other side. Closer . . . closer . . . then a gust of wind knocks me sideways and I'm blown off the tree trunk, my arms and legs flailing as I land in the angry river.

The cold hits me like an ice axe. I can't move. I can't breathe. I'm sinking. The waters have finally won . . .

My white skirt billows round my body as I sink in slow motion.

In my mind I see Moon-Star in his white beekeeping suit. He's smiling, and telling me, 'Swim, Queen Bee, swim to the moon . . .' So I force my arms and legs to move. THE WATERS SHALL NOT WIN. I kick up, up, up, towards the sky, towards Great-Gran Beatrix's star. I'm doing it, Moon-Star, I'm swimming to the moon!

I surface, spluttering. I try to move further along the tree, but my Marilyn skirt is snagged on a branch. It won't budge, so I yank at the flimsy material, ripping it. I'm free! My legs thrashing in the water, I drag myself from branch to branch along the tree, one at a time, until I reach the top branch. I'm a lot further away from the opposite bank than I thought.

I will have to swim again. I've got to save baby Daniel.

My swirly-swirly skirt wraps around me in

the water as I do my doggy-paddle. I start to count, and my legs splash, trying to kick. I get to eleven.

'Come on, Bee,' I say in my head. 12, 13, 14, 15, 16, 17, 18, 19, 20. I'm nearly there. Then a gush of water starts to pull me away from the bank and I have to fight it with every bit of strength left in me. As I get to twenty-five, my feet hit mud and I crawl up on to the opposite side. The elephant's waiting for me. I wheeze. But my inhaler is in the car.

Go, elephant, go! I think.

My bones hurt and my teeth are rattling as my body shakes from cold.

'Bee, Bee!'

I turn to see Dad on the opposite bank.

'I'm going to get Old Alice!' I call, as loud as I can, but he doesn't hear me as another tree comes crashing down behind him.

'DAD!' I scream. But he is OK, so I turn and force myself on, towards the clearing.

The fence has blown down. I step over the barbed wire, wincing as I step on the wire mesh, until I feel mud and grass beneath my toes. Dragging myself to the Promise Tree, I fling my arms round the trunk to gather a last bit of strength, then I force myself on again, past the empty hives and on down the path. There's wire and trunks and broken branches everywhere. It would have taken so long to steer the red wagon and Bob through all this. I cling to the hope that they haven't gone far.

By the time I reach the road out of the village, the elephant's stamping on my chest. I can't go much further. I can't.

A puddle is filling in a long groove ahead. It's a track . . . a wagon-wheel track . . . and hoof prints . . .

A neigh echoes through the air. Bob! I race on, and there, up ahead, stopped at the roadside, I see him, rearing up and pawing at the wind and rain. The red wagon and the Daisymobile are stopped there too.

'Moon-Star,' I whimper and then I shout with all my might, 'MOOON-STAAAARRRRRR!'

29

The wagon door opens. Moon-Star stands on the top step, his white shirt flapping in the wind. He sees me through the sheets of rain, and leaps down from the wagon, running towards me. I stagger on, my arms reaching for him.

He hugs me tight.

'Please, you've got to come, it's Chrystal's baby brother,' I wheeze, as Moon-Star practically carries me towards the wagon and up the steps.

Old Alice is waiting inside. Moon-Star puts me on a stool and Old Alice turns on the steamer and as I breathe in and out Moon-Star wraps a blanket round my shoulders. Once the wheezes stop, I tell them about baby Daniel and the collapsed bridge and the fallen tree.

Old Alice fills the pockets in her apron with herbs from the jars. Moon-Star disappears down the wagon steps, back out into the storm.

A fearful thought gives me a jolt. In my panic to find them, I hadn't thought about the journey back.

'How are we going to get you across the river, Old Alice?'

'There'll be a way . . . you'll see,' she mutters.

Daisy appears in the doorway with a sheet of plastic and a long rope. 'My boy's told me about the baby. I'm ready.'

Then comes a pounding of hooves and a thundering neigh.

Old Alice and I climb down the wagon steps. Moon-Star dismounts from Bob and gives Old Alice a leg up on to the horse's back. I clamber up behind Old Alice, holding on to her waist.

'I'm going in the Daisymobile with Ma,' Moon-Star tells us. 'Ride through the trees behind the Dog and Duck, then Bob won't have to walk over the wire fence. See you at the riverbank. Go on, boy, go.'

He pats Bob on the hind and we gallop off

through the wind and the rain. The Daisymobile passes us and I hold on to Old Alice for all I'm worth. It feels like we might get blown off Bob's back at any second. The trees whizz past, and then I hear the roar of the river as we approach it.

The Daisymobile is parked up in the trees ahead. Bob slows down to a trot, then prances around on the spot.

Fear grips me. 'What are we going to do?' I cry.

'You'll see,' says Old Alice.

An end of a rope is already tied to the Daisymobile's bumper. Moon-Star dives into the water and swims a powerful breaststroke to the tree that's crashed across the river. He ties the other end of the rope to a branch and swims back. The cold water doesn't seem to bother him at all.

'Ma, give me your pinny,' says Daisy as she climbs out of the camper van.

Old Alice unties her apron and hands it to Daisy, who wraps it in the plastic sheet and gives it to Moon-Star.

'Precious herbs in there,' Daisy says to him. 'Mustn't get them wet.'

'Bee,' says Moon-Star, 'it'll be too much for Bob to take both of you together. Can you keep these herbs out of the water as you go across? Gran'll need both hands to keep ahold of Bob. Get as far as you can – I'll come back for ya.'

I nod and swivel round to dismount Bob and grab the plastic bundle of herbs from Moon-Star.

'Come on, Bob, come on, boy,' he says, and he leads Bob down the bank. Bob shies.

'Whoa there,' soothes Moon-Star, then the brave horse and his brave master wade into the river with Old Alice on Bob's back.

I slide down the muddy bank on my bottom and the iciness of the water hits me again. I grab hold of the rope.

'Be brave, darling Bee,' shouts Daisy.

I lift the bag of herbs high in the air with my right hand, and with my left I grab and pull, grab and pull myself along the rope, beside the tree, then reach out and grab it further along and pull again. My frozen legs are kicking, thrashing, propelling my shivering body along. I look up and can just make out through the rain that Bob, Moon-Star and Old Alice have reached the far bank.

Moon-Star lifts his gran down from Bob and wades back into the water until he is swimming next to his horse. When he reaches me, he turns Bob around in the water so he is facing back towards the far bank and Little Ash. Then he grabs the bundle of herbs and, with a mighty throw, sends it hurtling through the air. It lands on the bank, not far from Old Alice's feet.

'You ready, Bee?' Moon-Star asks.

I nod and grab Bob's mane with my right hand, letting go of the rope with my left. As I hold on to the mane for dear life, my body floats up, up, up, over the horse's back. Moon-Star, Bob and I swim until we reach the far bank, my Marilyn dress floating in the water around me. Then Bob finds his feet and Moon-Star guides him up the slippery bank to where Old Alice is waiting, the apron of herbs back around her waist. Moon-Star gives Old Alice a leg up on to

Bob, then carefully guides us all through the fallen trees, to Duck Street and Chrystal's house.

'Whoa, Bob, whoa,' Old Alice calls as we reach the Kellys', pulling on the reins.

Bob stops, stamping his feet and snorting. I swing myself down and hold my arms out to Old Alice as she slides off the horse. She hitches up her skirts and runs through the front door, trailing water.

'Up the stairs,' I call.

I stumble into the nursery behind Old Alice.

Chrystal is scrunched up in the corner, crying into Lorna's shoulder. Dad is sitting next to Mum with his head in his hands.

'Bee!' Mum says. 'Oh, Bee, I've been out of my mind!'

They both run to me but I push through them.

'Let Old Alice see Daniel,' I say. 'She can help, I know she can.'

Mayor Kelly jumps up from his chair. 'NO!' he shouts, before Old Alice even has a chance to move.

'Let her,' Mrs Kelly begs her husband, rocking Daniel in her arms. He looks limp. 'Please.'

'Give me the bairn,' says Old Alice gently and she reaches out for him.

'Fetch me a blanket, child,' Old Alice says to me.

'Please, please help my brother,' sobs Chrystal.

I grab a blanket from Daniel's cot and spread it out on the floor. Old Alice lays Daniel on to the blanket, and Moon-Star puts out her herbs beside him. The baby is breathing, but his eyes are closed and he is very still.

Old Alice gently places her hands on Daniel, feeling his legs and arms and unbuttoning his little Babygro to look at his chest – just like she did with me. She mutters under her breath all the time. 'I need ice if you have it,' she says. Mum and Lorna rush out of the room to get some.

There is silence as everyone watches Old Alice mix her herbs in a saucer, making soothing sounds to baby Daniel, who still does not move.

His breath rattles.

'What good is this doing?' snaps Mayor Kelly.

'Shh! It's the only hope we've got,' sobs Mrs Kelly.

'I'll thank ye both to keep calm, for the bairn's sake,' says Old Alice sharply.

Mum and Lorna come back with a bucket of ice, blankets and Chrystal's fluffy pink dressing gown, which Mum makes me put on. I didn't even realise I was shivering. Dad peels off his jumper.

'Put that on, son,' he says, handing it to Moon-Star.

Mum drapes a blanket around Old Alice's shoulders. She doesn't look up but carries on putting a poultice of herbs on Daniel's chest, laying her hand on his body and talking to him.

'Come on, little one, come on. Come back to us.'

Many minutes pass; everyone is holding their breath. Then a glimmer of colour returns to Daniel's face. He shudders, opens his eyes and starts to cry.

He's come back.

30

I stand in front of my mirror, swirling around, admiring the new Marilyn dress that Old Alice has made me.

She's made it a bit bigger where my bumps should be.

'You'll grow into it,' she said, winking at me.

I put on my new DM boots and my bowler hat with the white silk daisy. I tilt the bowler back with such dazzling style that Great-Gran Beatrix would be extra proud. Then I drape the red feather boa over my arms and pick up the trilby with the feather. Now I'm ready.

Dad and Mum wait at the bottom of the rickety stairs, smiling as they watch me walk down.

I step out of the front door and I *don't* close my eyes. The old people from the Rise and Shine Happy Care Home for Older People are lining the pavement, clapping. Some are in wheelchairs, some are standing. Matilda, Mabel, Sid, Millie and Linford all send up a cheer. The old people follow as we parade down the middle of the road, past the Russian-doll houses, to the biggest one at the end of the street.

Mayor Kelly stands next to Mrs Kelly, who is carrying Mitzi. Today they are dressed in matching flowery dresses and straw hats. Chrystal is next to them, holding Daniel and giving him little kisses on the top of his head. Daniel breaks into a gummy smile when he sees me, but Chrystal does not look up. Lorna gives me a wink from where she stands, behind Chrystal. Apart from Chrystal, they all clap as I walk past, then they join the parade.

We head on towards the bridge, which has been rebuilt. When we cross it, I am proud that I do not have to hop but instead march proudly with my head held high. I never need to count to twenty-five ever again because I know the waters aren't going to get me.

Through the forest to the clearing we go. I see the red wagon and the Daisymobile through the trees. The fence has completely gone. Old Alice is sitting on the steps, puffing at her pipe, and Daisy is filling a bucket of water from the tap. She gives me a wave.

They both join the parade as we walk down the path. When we reach the empty hives, a hushed silence falls.

Moon-Star is walking towards us as slowly as a spaceman walking on the moon. He is dressed in his beekeeper's suit and in his hand is a broken-off branch with a cluster of bees attached to it. He carries it with such care that my heart melts.

When he reaches me, he smiles through the veil of his beekeeping suit and nods. I reach out and gently-gently-gently touch the bees. They are so warm and soft. Beautiful, beautiful bees.

No one moves, no one speaks, as Moon-Star places the branch with the cluster of bees into one of the hives.

Then we gather round the trunk of the Promise Tree, in front of the old plaque with the ancient myth. Mayor Kelly clears his throat, and reads the words aloud.

Behold the ancient pact of the town of Ashton. In the reign of King James, a bond was made betwixt the mayor of Ashton and those who travel betwixt dell and dale, on the day the mayor's beloved baby daughter, Elizabeth, was saved from the waters by the travellers. From this day forth, travelling folk shall be free to rest in the clearing by the hives in the wood and shall live in peace and harmony with the bees and nature.

Should this bond be broken, the bees will swarm and all the flowers and crops shall perish.

There is a blue velvet curtain hanging on the tree below it. Mayor Kelly draws it aside with a flourish and a new plaque is unveiled.

Moon-Star steps forward and slowly begins reading. He stumbles and halts but my heart swells with pride at each new word he utters.

'A bond was made between the mayor of Ashton and Old Alice, Daisy and Moon-Star Higgins, that travelling people shall rest in the clearing by the hives in the wood, and shall live in peace and harmony with the bees and nature. This bond was made on the day the mayor's beloved son Daniel was saved by Old Alice, with her ancient knowledge of herbs and the healing of her hands. Should this bond be broken, the bees will swarm and all the flowers and crops shall perish.'

Mayor Kelly shakes Old Alice's hand and claps Moon-Star on the shoulder.

As we turn to walk back up the path to the clearing, I see my whole class. They're being bossed about by Mrs Partridge, who has some sort of weird flowery hat on her head. Her little bald husband is leaning against a birch tree looking stressed. Mr and Mrs Gregory stand together, holding hands and smiling at me.

I wave hello.

Moon-Star climbs out of his beekeeping suit and stands there in the new jeans and stylish white shirt that Mum made Dad buy to thank him for teaching me to swim. I step forward and put the trilby with the feather on Moon-Star's head and we walk to stand beside Old Alice and Bob in a line.

Mayor Kelly makes a speech.

'Never have I met such a brave young lady as Bee Edwards. She fought through the worst storm the village has ever known, swimming across the river and risking her own life to bring help to my son. The bravery of Old Alice, Moon-Star and this fine horse Bob, who also crossed the river to reach Daniel, has left me truly humbled. I have been ignorant and prejudiced and putting up the fence nearly cost me my son's life. Today, I would like to show my appreciation. First, Old Alice.' He pins a pair of golden healing hands to her shawl. 'I also give you a little comfort to watch the sunset.'

Alfie and Burt stagger, sweating and arguing,

into the clearing, carrying a bench with a golden plaque that reads:

> For Old Alice,
> with thanks from Mayor Kelly.
> May she relax on this bench
> for the rest of her days.

'Moon-Star Higgins,' says Mayor Kelly, 'I applaud your bravery.' And he pins a gold moon to Moon-Star's shirt.

Then Mayor Kelly pats Bob on the nose and holds up a golden shiny horseshoe, which Bob tries to eat, so Moon-Star pins it to his bridle.

'And finally, to Bee.' And he pins a gold bee to my dress. It glistens in the sunlight. It's another all-time best moment in my life.

Everyone cheers and claps, Daisy whoops and twirls round in circles, then Dad steps out of the crowd and stands next to me. He coughs, then starts talking.

'Ladies and gentlemen, I am ashamed to say

that I laughed at my daughter when she entered the sponsored swim. I didn't think she could do it. Well, she proved me so wrong. Not only did she swim ten lengths in the pool, she swam across that dangerous river to save Daniel. Now, I ask for her forgiveness.'

Dad hands me a parcel wrapped in stripy black-and-yellow paper.

I open it slowly and there, nestled in the paper, is a shiny silver mobile phone.

I take a big breath, lock eyes with Dad and I don't have to dig deep in my scrapbook for a facial expression because I know my smile says it all. It is real as real can be and I am not acting.

I turn to face the crowd. 'My name is Beatrix Daffodil Tulip Chrysanthemum Rose Edwards and I want to thank you all for coming here today.' Then the words run out, so I just smile a happy smile at everyone in front of me. They smile right back.

Gradually the clearing empties as people start to drift off home. Old Alice disappears into the red wagon with Daisy, and Mum and Dad walk away through the trees, calling out that they will see me at home.

Something brushes against my leg. It's the grey kitten. I pick him up, give him a snuggle and send him on his way too.

Just as it looks as if everyone has gone, except for Moon-Star, Bob and me, Chrystal steps out from behind a tree. Bob startles and rears up. I stumble backwards in surprise and land on my bottom.

'Whoa, boy. Whoa,' says Moon-Star. He leads Bob away from Chrystal and me.

I'm not hurt. Chrystal holds out a hand to help me up, but I do not take it. I scramble to my feet on my own.

She holds out a pink package.

'It's for you, Bee. I was horrible to you, but you saved my brother's life. I'm really, really sorry.'

I stare at the package but don't take it from her.

'Go on,' she says. 'Open it. Double-dare you . . .'

I rip open the paper and inside is a furry bumblebee case for my mobile.

We look at each other and grin.

'You swim like a dog,' she says.

'Bendy tap-dancing freak,' I say.

Then Chrystal does a cartwheel and runs away from me, laughing.

'Over the rainbow and back,' I call after her.

Moon-Star trots over on Bob and pulls me up on to the horse's back. We gently ride round and round and round and I never want it to stop cos I know what's coming and I can hardly breathe.

Bob stops to eat some grass. Moon-Star slides off and lifts me down.

'Please,' I say. 'Please don't say it.'

'Hush, Bee.' Moon-Star puts a hand on my shoulder. 'I'm a traveller; it's what I do. You know I can't stay here, don't ya?'

I nod and blink, so no tears escape.

'I got to go with my ma – she needs me.'

I nod again, swallowing hard. I absolutely mustn't cry.

'You teaching me to read has given me my freedom,' Moon-Star continues. 'They're letting me go with Daisy now that I done some book learning. As long as I go to school when I can and Ma keeps me learning my lessons when I can't.'

We link thumbs and walk down the path to the Promise Tree. Moon-Star takes off the trilby and hands it to me.

'No, keep it please,' I say. 'Then I know you'll come to give it back to me some day.'

'I'll be back to visit,' he says and his lips brush my cheek. It's a barely-there whisper of a kiss, but I feel it.

Then he bends down and picks up a sharp stone and together we carve in the bark:

Moon-Star and Bee

Dear Moon-Star,

Here is a bee book like Great-Gran Beatrix
gave me. It is for you to write your thoughts in
when you are on the road in the Daisymobile.

Love,

Bee x

The thoughts of Moon-Star Higgins, from the Daisymobile

I, Moon-Star, am a man of my word. Every summer, when the honeybees needs harvesting, I come back to Ashton. First thing I does is climb up to Bee's window and she's there, sitting at her fancy dressing table, waiting for me in her Marilyn dress and her bowler hat. The dress is getting a bit small for her now but she won't part with it.

There is always a big grey cat on her lap. The little kitten is all grown-up now. It kept following Bee home till one day it stayed. She calls it Toto.

When Bee sees me, she smiles her pretty smile and I helps her out of the window and down to Bob and we rides through the village. Then we put on our beekeeping suits and harvest the bees with Gran watching. Her bones is getting really old now.

I get jars of honey for all the old people at the Rise and Shine Happy Care Home and I, Moon-Star, always label the jars 'Linford' and 'Millie' and 'Mabel' and so on and so on. Only there's no Sid any more, as he's parted this earth. I do all the labels cos I'm really good at my letters now.

When we've had tea at the Rise and Shine, we rides back to the woods to our special pool and we swim with Bob, then we lie back on the grass, looking at the starry sky, searching for Great-Gran Beatrix's star. It's always there twinkling down at us.

Thank you for reading.
Moon-Star Higgins

Acknowledgements

First thanks has to go to my editors, Naomi Greenwood and Emma Goldhawk, for helping me dive in and swim through the wild words of *Swimming to the Moon*, and for helping me shape those wild words into the story I wanted to tell. To Michelle Brackenborough for the absolutely gorgeous cover and designs throughout the book. Having a horse on the front cover is a childhood dream come true! And, to everyone at Hodder Children's Books – thank you for your amazing support.

Thank you to Katarina Jovanovic and Stephanie Allen for all things publicity – your hard work is so appreciated. To Caitlin Lomas, for all the groundwork you put in. Just keep swimming, Caitlin! To Jodie Hodges, my one in a million agent, and the amazing team at United Agents – Jane Willis, Emily Talbot and Kat Aitken. Thanks for always just being there.

To the friends who got me through the long writing hours – Christopher Ryan for being my first reader, Tracey Smith for being such a lovely friend, Jennifer Elson, Marcia Mantack, Sharon D. Clarke and Clare Calder, for your never ending belief and support, Adrian Ramagge, for doing my author PowerPoint presentation so beautifully, my fellow authors Hilary McKay and Steve Antony, for your huge encouragement and for making me laugh so much, Lou Kuenzler and City Lit, and my Festival Hall workshop group.

This book would not have been written without the support of Kentish Town City Farm. To Simone Uncle and Rachel Schwartz – thank you for letting me write at the farm. It's the perfect space to write, with the accompaniment of horses whinnying, chickens clucking, pigs and geese and dogs and all the other farmyard noises. To Diane Probets and Claire Probets Evans, a big thank you for all things horse-related. To Kerry Kennedy for being so supportive and just getting it – hurrah for dyslexics!

Huge thanks go to Tom Moggach the bee man, who I met the day of the swarm one May. Thank you for letting me walk down the grassy path to the hives and watch you at work. And, thank you for answering my endless questions. The book *Bees, Hives, Honey!: Beekeeping for Children* by Tim Rowe was also so helpful.

During my research, I learned that if bees are in a cluster and really calm, they don't mind being touched gently. But, it's always best **not** to touch the bees like Bee does in *Swimming to the Moon*, unless you are with an experienced bee-keeper.

A special thank you to the National Theatre costume department for letting Emma and I have a lovely afternoon trying on vintage hats. Feeling the textures, smelling the scents of days gone by, experiencing how the hats made me stand tall and gave me dazzling style really helped me get into the head of Bee!

Big thanks to Matthew McDowall, for sharing stories of *Ali Baba* – the pantomime he wrote and directed with the travelling community – and for giving me such insight. To Lisa Goldman and Susie McKenna, for your warm advice and for pointing me in the right direction when I started this project. To my dad, Brian Elson, who didn't think I could swim. Dad, it only made me determined to prove you wrong – thanks for coughing up all the sponsorship money! To Doris Barry and Bridget Espinosa, for trying in vain to teach me to curtsey gracefully.

To Marilyn Monroe and Judy Garland, whose stars still shine so brightly. I do hope you like being in *Swimming to the Moon*. Thanks also to Ian Dewar for his knowledge of Marilyn's films.

And finally, to Winston, the most beautiful, most gentle giant of a horse that ever lived! Big thanks to Harriet Smith, for taking the beautiful photograph of him for my biography, to Jack Hopson, for all the work you did with Winston, and to Alia Cooper, Winston's owner, for loving him and bringing out his full potential.

Winston – in the true spirit of *Swimming to the Moon*, you are proving all those who thought cob horses shouldn't do dressage wrong. You show them!

I dedicate this book to the memory of Warwick, my own free-spirited Moon-Star.